EMILY'S
ART AND SOUL

EMILY'S
ART AND SOUL

by

Joy Argento

2019

EMILY'S ART AND SOUL
© 2019 By Joy Argento. All Rights Reserved.

ISBN 13: 978-1-63555-355-0

This Trade Paperback Original Is Published By
Bold Strokes Books, Inc.
P.O. Box 249
Valley Falls, NY 12185

First Edition: January 2019

Credits
Editor: Lynda Sandoval
Production Design: Stacia Seaman
Cover Design by Joy Argento and Melody Pond

Acknowledgments

First and foremost, I would like to thank Kate Klansky. Your unending support and belief in me has meant everything. I've said it before and I'll say it again, my life is so much better with you in it.

Thank you to my editor, Lynda Sandoval, for all your help and your gentleness as we went through this process together. You have taught me so much, and I hope this book is just the beginning of many years working together.

Thank you to my kids Jamie, Jessica, and Tony, for allowing me the time to write when you were younger and for your encouragement now that you are adults. I am very proud of the people you have become. Special thanks to Jamie for telling me I was crazy when I needed to hear it.

Georgia Beers, thank you not only for your friendship but for all your words of encouragement and your willingness to answer my endless questions. I appreciate you more than you know.

My eternal gratitude goes to the following people, who were kind enough to be my first readers and tell me the truth about my writing. They are brave souls.

Barbara * Amy * Jenny * Bunny * Leah * Jackie * Julie

Thank you to my friends Karin Cole and Ellen Eassa for all your support.

I am so thankful to Sandy Lowe and the staff at Bold Strokes Books for welcoming me into the family.

This book wouldn't have been possible without my brother Charlie in my life. He was born with Down syndrome, and my parents were told by doctors that he would be a burden to us and should be put in an institution. They couldn't have been more wrong. Down syndrome children are pure love. He has been a blessing and a joy.

This book is dedicated to Chris Waara.
She is the first person who told me I should write.
Although I don't think this is what she had in mind.

CHAPTER ONE

I gonna cook some breakfast. Want me make you some?"

"You know how to cook?" Emily asked her sister.

"Sure! I not a dummy, you know. Toast is my sp-sp-specialty." She blinked hard as if she had to force the last words out as her thick tongue got in the way. Having Down syndrome sometimes made talking difficult.

This was the second of many mornings that Emily and Mindy would share together. Emily wasn't sure how this was going to work out. Suddenly sharing her new home with her mentally challenged younger sister had never been on her life's to-do list. Of course, neither was getting a divorce or moving to a new town. Seems like there were a lot of things happening lately that were not on her list.

"No thanks, honey. I'll just have some coffee. But you go ahead and make yourself something to eat." The thought of putting food in her stomach made her feel even queasier than her nerves did.

"Mom always told us breakfast is the most im-port-ant meal of the day, ya know." The word sounded more like "bweakfast" when Mindy said it.

"I know, Mindy," Emily said, sitting down at the kitchen table with the newspaper and her coffee. "I'll eat something in a little while." She kept one eye on her little sister as she made herself toast and scrambled eggs, surprised by how well she managed. Emily didn't know how much of the credit went to their mother and how much of it Mindy learned at the special school she had attended. The school was primarily for kids like Mindy with learning disabilities. *Is that even correct to say? Is "mentally challenged" correct?* Emily had a hard time keeping up with what was politically correct or not these days.

The school taught life skills like cooking, laundry, and taking the bus, along with the basics of math, reading, and writing. Mindy's quick smile earned her a lot of friends there, but she had to leave them all behind to make the move from Rochester to Syracuse with Emily, eighty miles away in the heart of New York State. A lot of things change when your mother dies.

"So, what are you planning on doing when you get home today?" Emily asked when Mindy sat down at the table with her food.

"I gonna send out b-birthday cards."

"Oh yeah? Who are you sending them to?"

"My friends, Jill and Tommy. Their birthdays are Thursday. They have the same birthday as Michael Jackson."

Emily wasn't sure what to say. She ran a hand through her hair as she thought for a moment. She looked at her sister, toying with the idea of not saying anything. They had just lost their mother. Should she tell her that Michael Jackson was also dead? *Better she hears it from me than from someone else.* She reached for Mindy's hand across the table. "You know Michael Jackson died, don't you?"

"Of course," Mindy said, rolling her eyes. "I not sending *him* a card!" She laughed.

Relieved, Emily laughed too.

❖

Emily stared at herself in the mirror. She looked much better than she felt. This was the first time in eight years that she was starting a new job, and her stomach wasn't taking the change well.

"I hate this," she said out loud. She smiled wide—actually it was more like a grimace—and leaned in toward the mirror to inspect her recently brushed teeth. Satisfied, she poured a little mouthwash into a Dixie cup and swished it around her mouth. *Don't want my new coworkers hating me because of bad breath, now do I? If they are going to hate me, they are going to have to come up with a better reason.*

"What are you talking about?" she asked her reflection. "Of course they're going to like you. They're going to love you. They love people who talk to themselves." She brushed her fingers through her hair, trying to puff up her bangs. The light brown color was inherited from her mother; she wished she had gotten some of the curl as well. "It's the people who answer themselves that you have to watch out for. Right?" More finger strokes. "Right!" she said under her breath. She let out a long sigh. *It's going to be all right.*

Who wouldn't love you? Well, there was Brian. Brian didn't love you. Her mind went to her husband—ex-husband. The divorce would be final in a few days. She doubted Brian had ever loved her. At this point, she was pretty sure she had never loved him either. Why had she even married him? Because he was the first and only man that she'd ever had any feelings for. At the time, she had mistaken them for love. Now she realized the feelings had been more of comfort and security.

Love. She had never felt true love for any of the men she dated. None of them stirred any real feelings in her at all. Not one of them made her heart beat faster or gave her butterflies in the stomach. Not Brian and not Mark, nor any of the boys she'd dated in high school.

Still a virgin at twenty-one, Emily thought it was about time to experience that thing they wrote about in songs. Making love. Intercourse. Coitus. Sex. She'd put it off long enough. Mark had looks that could make any woman swoon. Well, *almost* any woman. Six months of dating and Mark's gentle prodding and she finally gave in. It wasn't horrible, but she didn't hear the angels singing either. She'd slept with Mark more out of curiosity about sex than desire. She broke up with him the next day.

That was fourteen years ago. Since then, she'd slept with a few different men, and while she didn't dislike it, she never understood what all the fuss was about. She married Brian when she was twenty-eight. Without much discussion, they'd waited until their wedding night to have sex. That had been fine with Emily, and apparently, it had been fine with Brian too. Now Emily wondered why.

Emily shook the memories away. She needed to finish getting ready or she was going to be late for her first day at the new job. She buttoned up her white blouse and smoothed out her dress pants with her hands. Dressing up was not something she enjoyed, but she thought she should look presentable today. She could dress down on the weekend. *Don't think about the weekend. Let's just get through today.* This was the start of her new life and she wanted to do it right.

"Are you almost done in there?"' Mindy knocked on the door. "I have to get ready too, ya know."

Emily made a mental note to pick up a shower curtain for the main bathroom after work today. They had most of the house furnished and decorated, but a few small things still needed to be done. Mindy had been using Emily's bathroom to shower, and while Emily didn't mind, she thought Mindy would appreciate having her own shower to use.

Emily opened the door. Mindy looked her up and down. "You look bea-u-tiful." She patted Emily on the back.

"You're a doll. I needed that." Emily gave her little sister a hug, bending to do it. Mindy was a good five inches shorter than Emily's five foot six. Despite being shorter, Mindy weighed a little more than Emily's 130 pounds, giving her a full face and a little pudge around the belly.

"You know you are my f-f-favorite sister." Mindy pushed a

chunk of blond hair away from her big blue eyes and smiled at Emily.

Emily brushed her fingers through the section of hair that Mindy had just moved and gently pushed Mindy's pink-rimmed glasses farther up on her nose. "I am your only sister, silly."

"Well, even if I had a million, billion sisters, you would be my bestest one! Now go to work so you don't be late."

"Bossy, bossy," Emily said. "Tell me again. What time are you getting picked up?"

"Nine thirty."

"And what's the name of the person picking you up?"

"Cindy. I think I'll call her Cindy Snickerdoodle." Mindy giggled. "I just kiddin' you," she said, with a crooked-toothed grin. "Cindy Sams. But I like Cindy Snickerdoodle better."

"Okay, okay, I have to get going. Do you need anything before I leave?"

"Nothing, nothing, nothing. Now, go to work." Mindy waved Emily away from the bathroom.

Emily gathered a few items and put them into a small backpack. She heard the shower turn on, and above the hum of the water she could make out the sound of Mindy singing. Emily smiled to herself. They had both been through a tremendous amount of change in the last two months, but they were going to get through it and come out the other side stronger. Emily was sure of it.

Cindy "Snickerdoodle" was picking Mindy up in an hour to give her a ride to Mirique Works, a program set up by the county to provide "special needs" adults with jobs skills, a social outlet, and eventually a job. Mindy had belonged to a similar program in Rochester.

Mindy didn't seem to mind living with Emily or the fact that they'd moved to another city. Emily did her best not to hover and do too much for her. When Mindy was living with Mom and Dad, they'd let her do a lot of things for herself. They knew she could handle it. But Mom died two months ago, and Dad decided that drinking and sleeping all day was the best way to handle his grief. When Emily decided it was better for Mindy to come and live with her, their father had no objections.

Emily had already sold the house she'd shared with Brian and bought a new one in Syracuse when Mindy came to live with her. The old job was behind her and the new one had already been lined up. She promised Mindy they would go back to Rochester often to visit. There was no doubt Mindy would make new friends here. Her smile and bubbly personality easily won people over.

A change-of-life baby. That's what Mom had called Mindy. She was forty-five and Emily was thirteen by the time Mindy surprised everyone with her birth. Emily loved her baby sister, but life was busy for the teenager. Between school, her friends, and track practice, she had very little time to really get to know her. Emily left for college the week Mindy turned six. She was starting to get to know her now and was very glad about that.

Emily grabbed her backpack and keys and ducked out the side door into the garage. Sliding into the driver's seat of her Volkswagen Golf, she realized that she was still nervous but less nauseous. *You would think that by the age of thirty-five you wouldn't feel like it was your first day of high school all over again.* She slowly backed out of the garage and headed toward her new job at Freemont High, twenty minutes away.

❖

Emily left the school office juggling an arm full of paperwork and several small boxes of art supplies. She struggled with balancing the piles as she ambled down the long hall following the principal's directions to her art room. As she rounded a corner, the pile slid in her arms, and despite her best efforts to readjust her load, it slipped out of her grasp and scattered to the floor.

"Damn it," she said under her breath, as she squatted down to gather everything up.

"Sure. Your first day here, and you think you can dump

your stuff wherever you want?" It was a female voice she didn't recognize, but of course, she didn't really know anyone at the school yet.

Emily looked up. "I'm sor—I dropped—I'm trying—oh—geez."

The stranger knelt down beside her, picking up papers and paintbrushes. She paused long enough to extend a hand. "Hi. I'm Andi—Andi Marino." Her broad smile brought out deep-set dimples in her cheeks. "I didn't mean to startle you. I was just trying to be funny."

Emily shook her hand and looked into bottomless brown eyes. *Holy shit, she's pretty. Holy shit! Did I just think that?* Emily blushed and pushed the thoughts aside. She guessed the woman to be about her age, maybe a year or two older. Her brown hair was so dark that it was almost black and hung down a tad below shoulder length with the slightest bit of a curl at the end. The length was shorter in the front and it framed her face and soft features nicely. She wore no makeup, but then again, she didn't need any. Her skin had a natural glow and her eyes held a sparkle that lit up when she smiled.

"I teach math here." Andi handed Emily a stack of papers. They both stood, all of the papers and boxes now back in Emily's arms.

"Art. Art teacher. I'm the new art teacher," she stammered.

"I thought you might be," Andi said, as she slipped several paintbrushes into one of the boxes. "Do you have a name or should I just refer to you as 'the art teacher'?" She made air quotes with her fingers.

Emily noticed that the dark jeans and light blue polo shirt Andi wore hugged her slim body but showed off curves in all the right places. *I'm going to have to find out about the dress code for teachers around here. I would much rather be wearing jeans.*

"I'm sorry. I'm kind of flustered, this being my first day and all. I'm Emily Sanders."

"No need to get flustered yet. Most teachers wait until the

students arrive to do that. They'll keep you on your toes, for sure." Andi smiled. "This isn't your first year teaching, is it?"

"Oh, no. I taught at a school in Rochester for several years."

"You'll like it here. It's a great school with a great staff—well, mostly a great staff."

Emily raised her eyebrows. "Mostly a great staff?"

"Hmm, shouldn't have said that." Andi tilted her head and made a face. "Speaking of staff, we have a mandatory staff meeting in the auditorium in thirty minutes. Do you know where that is? Do you know your way around the school yet?"

"Let's see, I know where the main office is and the art room. So that would be a no. I don't know. I have a map here, somewhere..." The paper threatened to topple again as Emily shifted the load around in her arms in search of the map.

Andi helped her readjust one of the boxes. "If it would help, I can come by the art room in about twenty minutes, and we can go together. I can even give you a tour of the school afterward if you want."

"Oh my God. That would be wonderful. I would be so grateful."

"No problem. Do you know where you're going right now?" Andi asked.

"Yep. I go down to the end of this hall and turn left. Right? I mean, correct?"

"Yes, left, that's right—correct." Andi laughed. "That's the way to the art room all right. I'll see you in about twenty minutes." Andi turned and went in the opposite direction.

Emily watched her walk away, once again noticing the form-fitting jeans.

Once in the art room, Emily set her armload down on the closest table. She turned, hands on her hips, and surveyed the place. Several color charts and a few old, faded posters hung on the walls. Three deep sinks controlled by foot pedals sat side by side in the corner, and drawing tables were scattered about the room. Light streamed in through large windows, illuminating several large, well-worn wooden easels. On the wall behind her desk hung a small blackboard trimmed with light oak. The tray held several pieces of broken chalk in various colors, along with a dusty eraser. The chalkboard seemed out of place next to the brand new smart board, but Emily was sure she would use both. *Okay, I like this room. I can do this.* After a little rearranging and some new posters on the walls, she would like it even more.

Her thoughts were interrupted by a knock on the door. "It hasn't been twenty min—oh." It wasn't Andi.

The frown on the woman's face was less than welcoming. Her gray hair pulled tightly back from her face was twisted into a bun. Emily wondered how she was able to walk in the narrow, pointy-toed, high-heeled shoes that her feet were stuffed into. Her flower printed dress reminded Emily of something her grandmother would have worn—twenty years ago.

"Hi," Emily said, cheerfully and a bit hopefully.

"Mrs. Sanders?" Her voice was as stern as her face.

"*Miss* Sanders," she corrected. "Emily."

"*Miss* Sanders. You failed to sign some very important paperwork in the office." The woman's frown deepened. Any deeper and Emily was sure her face would crack.

"I was in the…" Emily stopped her explanation, realizing it was fruitless. Time to change tactics. "I am so sorry." She smiled sweetly. "Can I come by after the staff meeting to sign them?"

"I suppose that would be fine." One side of her mouth tilted up at an angle.

I wonder if that is her idea of a smile.

The woman nodded and was gone, probably off to harass someone else.

Emily went back to the task at hand: sorting through boxes of art supplies. She was lost in thought when Andi silently slipped into the room and came up behind her.

"Finding anything good?" Andi asked quietly.

"Holy shit!" Emily jumped, almost knocking into Andi. "Stop sneaking up on me. You're going to give me a heart attack." She turned with hand over her heart but couldn't help smiling.

"I'm so sorry." Somehow it didn't sound sincere through the giggle that Andi tried to suppress. "Oh, these are great." Andi thumbed through a pile of art posters lying on a table nearby. "I love art. I wish I was creative, but I can't even draw a straight line."

"That's one of the reasons they make rulers," Emily teased with a grin.

"Thanks." Andi grinned back, showing off a row of almost perfect white teeth. One tooth front and center in the bottom row leaned a bit to the left. Somehow Emily found that endearing. "I'll try to remember that. Are you ready for the meeting?"

"Let me get my stuff and I'll be set." She swung her backpack over one shoulder as she followed Andi out the door. Without her permission, Emily's eyes once again went to Andi's rear. *I wish my jeans looked that good on my butt.*

❖

Andi was glad that boring meeting was over. She had given Emily a quick tour of the school but was sure it would still take Emily a few days to figure out her way around. She sat comfortably on one of the drawing tables, swinging her legs back and forth, careful not to let her toes scrape the floor.

She watched as Emily dumped a box of paints onto a nearby table. "So, are you ready for the students to start in two weeks?" she asked. It was nice having someone new to chat with. She considered several of the teachers here friends, but there was something about Emily. She barely knew her but already felt comfortable being around her.

"Pretty much. I'm really looking forward to it. I still need to finish sorting out these supplies. How about you?"

"I have a calculator. That's all I need. At least that's what most of the kids think. They don't need to bother learning anything because they can just use the calculators on their phones. I tell ya, back when I was a kid, they didn't have calculators or smartphones. We were lucky if we had a pencil and paper to figure out math problems. And then we had to sharpen the pencils with our teeth, because pencil sharpeners hadn't been invented yet."

Emily separated the paints into piles. "I guess you should count yourself lucky you had that, because I hear the kids with stone tablets and chisels had it even worse. Those chisels were murder on the teeth."

"Ain't that the truth?" Andi slid off her perch and walked over to Emily. "Need any help?"

"Sure. If you're serious, can you sort the rest of these paints? Oil paints in that pile and watercolors over here." Emily pointed as she spoke.

"Okay then. What are you going to do while I do this?"

Emily sat down on the same table Andi had just vacated. Swinging her legs, she said, "I am going to sit here and watch you work for a while. Sorting is hard work and I need a rest." She lasted all of two minutes before getting up and grabbing a box of paintbrushes.

"All done resting?" Andi asked.

"Yep. I was wrong. I can't sit there and watch you work." Emily smiled. Her eyes crinkled a bit at the corners and Andi noticed how blue they were, even under the room's harsh fluorescent lights. She made a mental note to try to make this new friend smile more often.

CHAPTER TWO

Emily changed out of her dress clothes and into jeans and a T-shirt as soon as she got home. The casual clothes helped her relax.

"Did you make s-s-some new friends at school t-today?" Mindy's tone sounded more like she was asking a child starting kindergarten instead of her older sister starting a new job.

"As a matter of fact, I did." Emily handed her a couple paper napkins to put on the table for supper.

"Who?" Mindy asked.

"Let's see. I met the lady from the front office. I don't think we'll be really good friends, though, because I forgot to sign some papers, so she was kind of mad at me. And I met some people in the main office like the principal, and I talked to two teachers after the staff meeting. But the nicest person that I met today was Andi, the math teacher."

"Ooooh! Is he your boyfriend?" Mindy put her hand over her mouth and giggled.

Emily playfully swatted at her with a dishtowel. "No, silly. Andi is a girl. She showed me around the school, so now I won't get lost. Hopefully."

"What does she look like?"

Emily smiled. "She is a little bit taller than me. She has very dark brown hair, about down to here." Emily showed Mindy with her hand. "She has pretty brown eyes and dimples."

"Dimples." Mindy giggled. "What the heck is that?"

"Hmm, that's a good question. It's sort of like little holes in your face, right here." Emily pointed to her own cheeks.

"Can you see her teeth through the holes?" Mindy asked.

Emily laughed. "No, honey, the holes don't go all the way through her face. They only go in a little tiny bit. A dent more than a hole, I guess."

Emily donned an oven mitt and pulled a pan out of the oven. The room filled with the warm scent of tomato sauce and pepperoni. Frozen pizza definitely wasn't her idea of a healthy meal, but it was the best she could do after her first day of work. "So, how about you? Did you make any friends today?"

"I m-met lots of people today," Mindy started. Twenty minutes later Mindy was still talking between bites of her food. In great detail, she told Emily everything that had happened and about everyone she'd encountered. Two people, Daisy and Jeffrey, were now considered her new *best* friends.

Plunging into a bowl of vanilla ice cream for dessert, Mindy turned the topic of conversation to their mother.

"You really miss her, don't you?" Emily asked.

"I miss her a whole lot. She was the greatest m-mother in the whole world. I not so sure why people die. How come people die, Emily? Daddy said it was 'cause God wanted her with him. But I wanted her with me."

Emily reached across the table and took Mindy's pudgy hands in her own. "Oh, sweetie, I miss her too. Sometimes the bodies that we have stop working right, and we die. Like the blood vessel in Mom's head stopped working, and she died. Mom was lucky enough to have a wonderful place like heaven to go to. She's with God now and waiting for the rest of the people she loves to join her."

"Like us?"

"Like us. But that probably won't be for a very long time, so Mom has God and Grandma and Grandpa and Uncle Johnny to keep her company until it's our turn to join her. Do you understand?"

Mindy nodded. The look of confusion left her face. "We are so, so lucky, Emily. We had the b-b-bestest mom in the whole world and we had her for a long time, ever since I was a little baby, even. And she is okay now. She isn't in no pain, no more." Mindy shook her head.

Emily rose and gave Mindy a tight squeeze. When Mindy had enough of it, she gently pushed Emily away with a giggle. Emily roughed up her hair. She loved her baby sister, but it was surprising her how much she liked having her around.

"Okay, little girl, let's get these dishes done."

"Hey! I am not a little girl. If I am a little girl, you are an old lady." Her laugh came out more like a snicker.

"Okay, big girl, let's get these dishes done."

"Okay, okay, okay, that's better. You wash, I dry."

"How about we put them into this dishwasher here? It came with the house, ya know."

Mindy slapped her hand against her forehead. "Oh yeah, I forgot 'bout that. How do we do it again?"

Emily showed Mindy how to load the dishes, but her thoughts turned to Andi and she smiled. She looked forward to her new job if it included people like her.

CHAPTER THREE

It was the first day of school for the students, and Emily felt like it was her first day of work all over again. Her fingers tapped out a nervous rhythm on the steering wheel as she drove across town. She parked in the lot designated for teachers, and the sun warmed her skin as she got out of the car and breathed in the beautiful, early September day.

She knew she was ready. Staff meetings, curriculum planning, and organizing her classroom had kept her pretty busy the last couple of weeks. Her teaching plan was well thought out and clear. *Nothing to be nervous about.* She took another deep breath.

Compared to teaching at a city school in the heart of Rochester, this should be a piece of cake. She had gotten to know those kids, those tough inner-city kids, and they had come to respect her. She was starting over here. New school. New kids. *Fear of the unknown.* She realized the pattern in herself. This fear wasn't a new thing. She shook her head and half smiled at the revelation. Not that it made it any easier for her to walk into the two-story brick building and confront the unknown.

Once in her classroom, Emily let out a sigh, set her backpack on the desk, and proceeded to take the chairs off the tables. She didn't have to wait long for her homeroom students. A quiet buzz grew into loud chatter as the teenagers trickled in, forming small groups, clamoring to catch up on summer activities and the latest gossip.

Emily jumped as the bell, indicating the start of the school day, blasted over the loudspeaker above her head. "Everyone take a seat," she said, trying to cover her embarrassment. She repeated the command to a few stragglers who continued to chat.

"Good morning." Emily forced a smiled at the new faces. "I'm Miss Sanders. Obviously, I'm the new art teacher here, seeing as we are in the art room."

A few of the kids chuckled.

"Now that we know who I am, let's find out who you are. Please raise your hand when I call your name. Susan Abbott?" She looked around the room until her eyes found the hand raised in the air. Her eyes followed the hand down to the young girl's face. Emily knew it would take time, but she wanted to try to get a handle on matching names and faces. She marked her attendance sheet and read the next name. "Kenneth Anderson?"

The tension eased with each name she called. The butterflies in her stomach took flight and went on their merry way. The setting was new, but the routine was familiar, and she knew that soon, it would feel like home here. She was sure of it.

The day seemed to fly by, and before she knew it, the final bell rang, signaling the end of the last period. There were no lessons today. Instead, Emily talked to the kids about art and what they hoped to get out of the class. It had been a very productive day, and at the tail end of it, Emily sat at her desk sorting through her attendance sheets.

"Knock, knock." The sound of Andi's voice made her smile. "Hi there."

"Hi, yourself." Andi's smile matched her own as she leaned in the door. She wore a simple lavender pullover shirt and dark dress pants. Emily missed the jeans, but she looked great dressed up too. "How did it go today?"

"Excellent. I think it went really well. They seem like a great bunch. Of course, I know it was only the first day and everyone was on their best behavior." Emily gathered a few stray pens from her desktop and put them in the drawer.

"Yes. It doesn't hurt that art is an elective either. The kids that are in your class are here because they want to be. Not always the same story with my math students."

"True, but I also get the kids who think art is an easy A and don't want to put in the effort."

"Good point. Hey, I was wondering if you wanted to grab a cup of coffee or something. There's a decent place a few miles down the road. Good coffee. Great pastries."

Emily took a quick look at her watch. It would be a little over an hour before Mindy got home. She knew she would be fine by herself for a little while but didn't want to be too late getting home to make supper. "Sure," she said. "But I need to be home by five." Okay, she could be a little late getting home, if it meant spending time getting to know Andi.

"Got a hot date?"

"Yeah." Emily put some papers into her backpack as she rose. "A hot date with my sister."

❖

The coffee shop was bright and cheery as Emily followed Andi in. The aroma of fresh roast and baked goods permeated the air. The red and white checkered tablecloths gave the place an old-fashioned look and feel. A sign by the door informed them to seat themselves, and Andi led the way to a table by the window.

"This is a cute little place." Emily slid into the booth.

"Coffee?" The waitress, complete with a pink uniform and

pinafore apron, was at the table with a pot of coffee ready to pour. It looked like something you would see on an *I Love Lucy* rerun.

"Yes, thanks," Andi said, turning the coffee cup in front of her upright.

Emily copied the action and nodded.

The waitress filled both cups and set the pot down on the table. Reaching into the pocket in the front of the apron, she pulled out a green pad and pen. "Ready to order?" Her eyes were young but her skin showed too many days spent in the sun.

"What's good here?" Emily asked Andi.

"I love the Danish. Cheese is my favorite, but cherry comes in a close second."

"Ooh. Cherry sounds great. I'll have that, please."

Andi ordered the cheese Danish and the waitress was off.

Emily reached for the sugar and half-and-half. Andi watched with obvious amusement as she opened and poured four little containers of half-and-half and two packets of sugar into her coffee. Emily caught her eye. "What?" she asked.

"You like a little coffee with your cream and sugar?" Little laugh lines appeared around Andi's eyes with her smile.

"A little," Emily answered, enjoying the company. Andi had a great sense of humor and Emily had no trouble playing along.

Andi sipped her coffee—black.

Emily gave her coffee mixture several rotations with her spoon. Cherry filling oozed onto her plate as she cut into her pastry. Another couple of drops fell as she bit into the piece on her fork.

Andi reached across the small table, ran her finger across the drips, and put her finger into her mouth. Emily watched the movement with great interest. Andi looked up to see Emily watching her. "Sorry," she said, looking a little embarrassed. "I wanted to see how the cherry tasted. You can have a bite of my cheese Danish if you want." She cut a piece of her own food, stabbed it with her clean fork, and reached across the table, sliding it into Emily's open mouth.

"Mmm," was all Emily could say. She was too surprised by this whole exchange with her new friend to say much more. She had a few close friends back in Rochester, but none of them would have reached for that drip of filling or offered a bite of food to her off their own fork. She liked the way it felt. She liked this budding friendship. She had the feeling Andi would become a very good friend.

"So, tell me about this hot date you have with your sister. Is she your only sister? Do you have other siblings?" Andi took a bite of her pastry. "Isn't this food good?"

Emily took a sip of her diluted coffee before answering. "It's just supper at home, yes, no, and yes."

"Huh?"

"My hot date with my sister is just supper at home. Yes, she is my only sister. No, I don't have other siblings, and yes, this food is good. Really good!"

Andi laughed.

"Mindy came to live with me after our mom died a few months ago. Well, my mom died a few months ago, and my sister came to live with me a few weeks ago," Emily clarified.

"Oh, Emily. I am so sorry. Was it sudden?" Andi's face showed true concern.

"Yes. It was very sudden. Brain aneurysm. She was gone before we even knew what was happening."

"It must have been so hard for you." Andi reached across the table and squeezed Emily's hand. It radiated warmth, and Emily liked the comfort of it. Andi seemed to be waiting for Emily to continue.

"It was. I still miss her every day. But having my sister around helps. My dad was having trouble with his own grief, so we thought Mindy would be better off with me for now."

Andi let go of her hand. Emily missed the feeling of it immediately, but it didn't seem appropriate to reach for it back.

"How old is Mindy?"

"Twenty-three." Emily liked having someone to talk to,

someone who really seemed to care. "Mindy has Down syndrome. She's very self-reliant and what you would call high functioning, but she still needs someone to look after her. In many ways, she is like a child, and in some ways, she's more of an adult than I am. There is a wisdom about her that a lot of people don't have, and she is so full of love for everyone. I do my best to make sure she has what she needs."

"It's wonderful that you do that for her."

"I don't feel like I'm doing anything special. She's my sister. We take care of each other." Emily continued to eat and sip her coffee while she talked. "I like having her around. I like taking care of her, although she thinks I try to do too much. But she's a great kid—young woman. I guess she will always be a kid in a lot of ways."

"Sounds like you love her a lot."

"I do."

"So, your last name—Sanders. Is that English? Scottish?"

"Very good, I'm impressed. It is a Scottish name. But I am a mutt, Scottish, French, and Italian."

"Wow, your people really got around," Andi joked.

Emily couldn't help but laugh. "Yes, I guess you can say that. You're Italian, right?"

"Yep. One hundred percent."

That explains the beautiful brown eyes. "How long have you been teaching?" Emily took the last bite of her food.

"Hmm, let's see…this is my thirteenth year. Wow, does that make me feel old."

"Have you been at the same school the whole time?"

"Started here pretty much out of college and never left. I complain about the kids sometimes, but I do love it. The school district is good," Andi continued. "We have some great teachers. It's the school I graduated from."

"Wow!" Emily was surprised. "You didn't stray far from home, then. Did you go to college here too?"

"No, I went to college in Buffalo. I loved it there, but it didn't feel like home. You know?"

The waitress came back to refill their coffees. Emily put her hand over her cup and shook her head. She knew that any more caffeine and she would have trouble sleeping that night. Andi accepted the refill.

Emily waited until the waitress left before continuing her questions. "So, what about your personal life? Married? Boyfriend?" Emily noted that there were no rings on Andi's fingers.

"No," was her simple answer.

"Oh, you aren't getting off that easy. As pretty and friendly as you are, there must be someone special in your life." Emily couldn't believe someone hadn't snatched her up yet.

"Well, I ended a four-year relationship last year." Andi averted her eyes.

Emily thought maybe she had overstepped. "Oh, I'm sorry. I didn't mean to press. I am just interested in knowing more about you."

"No big deal. It simply wasn't working. I think the relationship really ended about a year before I left."

"So, what happened, if you don't mind me asking? How come it didn't work out? He just wasn't right for you?" Emily asked.

Andi hesitated. "*She*...is a nice person and we're still friends, but we weren't right together." She paused, her eyes never leaving Emily's.

Emily let the information sink in.

"Does it bother you that I'm gay?"

"Hmm. Well, to be honest, I'm a bit confused."

"I've heard the questions before. Yes, I'm sure and no, it isn't because I haven't met the right man yet. I get asked that a lot." Andi's voice was lighthearted but her eyes intense.

Emily assumed she was watching for her reaction. "No, that

wasn't what I was confused about." Emily sipped her coffee, forcing Andi to wait. "What confuses me is how come you teach math? Shouldn't you be a gym teacher?" She smiled at her own joke, hoping the humor would ease the tension she saw in Andi's eyes.

"Oh, aren't you just so funny?" Andi smiled back. "I was very nervous about telling you. I've lost a couple of friends in the past when I came out to them."

"They couldn't have been very good friends, then." Emily couldn't believe someone would pull away from Andi for that.

Andi seemed visibly relieved.

"Relax," Emily said, with a wink. "I know lesbians are almost like real people."

Andi shook her head. A smile lit up her face and she let out a laugh.

She's even prettier when she smiles. Emily was intrigued.

"Okay, so your turn now. Anyone special in your life?"

"Oh, no. We aren't done talking about you." She wanted to know more about this lovely woman sitting across from her.

"What else do you want to know?"

"Well, let's start with your name. Where did Andi come from? Did your dad want a boy?"

"Considering he already had four of them by the time I was born, I doubt it. I was named after his mother. My real name is Andreina. My mom was never crazy about that name but named me that because it was important to my father. Anyway, she's called me Andi since I was born. I like it much better. And just so you know, I don't usually tell people my real name."

"But you told me?"

"Must be because you're so easy to talk to."

Emily smiled. She found Andi easy to talk to as well.

The exchange continued freely until Andi glanced at her watch. "I hate to say it, but it's twenty to five. We need to get going if you are going to be home on time."

"Wow, the time flew by." Unexpected disappointment seeped

in. "Yes, I do need to get going. I have thoroughly enjoyed our conversation. Thank you."

"It was my pleasure. I'll walk you to your car."

Andi stopped at the cash register to pay the bill and refused to take the money Emily tried to hand her. "I've got it," she said. "We'll have to do this again sometime," she added.

"I would like that."

"How about this weekend? My place?"

"I look forward to it," Emily said. And she meant it.

Andi slid into her car and watched Emily do the same a few parking spots over. She let out an audible sigh. She never knew how someone would react when she came out to them, and Emily had responded in the best possible way.

She wasn't being overly dramatic when she told Emily that she'd lost friends over this. Mary Wilkins, her best friend since sixth grade, called her a lezzy, a dyke, and fucking liar when Andi came out to her halfway through her senior year in high school. When she asked Andi if she had feelings for her, Andi should have lied. But she didn't. She'd had feelings that she'd kept hidden for years. She confessed them to Mary. In return Mary told her the thought of Andi sleeping next to her all those times they'd had sleepovers made her want to vomit. She accused Andi of using her for her perverted fantasies. Andi would never make that mistake again. No. Nothing good could ever come from telling a straight girl you were in love with them.

The thought of that conversation—more like a one-way rant—still weighed heavy on Andi's heart, even after all these years. It definitely made her wary of sharing too much of herself with people. But Emily seemed different from most people. For whatever reason, Andi felt safe revealing her truth to Emily and letting the chips fall where they may. She knew there was a risk that Emily would run screaming and she would lose the possibility of friendship. But what good was a friendship if you couldn't be yourself anyway? But Emily hadn't run. In fact she made a joke, eliminating the possibility of tension. For that, Andi was grateful. They say the best way to a man's heart is through his stomach. Andi believed the best way to anyone's heart was through humor. Emily made her laugh, and Andi was already carving out a special place in her heart for her.

CHAPTER FOUR

"Hi there, come on in," Andi pushed the screen door open and stepped out of the way to let Emily pass. Emily noticed she smelled like warm vanilla spice, one of her favorite scents. She stopped in the foyer and looked around on the floor, doing her best not to smirk.

"What are you doing?" Andi asked.

"You don't have any cats?" Emily brought her eyes up to Andi's.

"Why? Are you allergic to cats?"

"No, I thought it was a prerequisite for lesbians."

Andi laughed. "You are just so funny, aren't you? No, it isn't a prerequisite." Almost as if on cue, Emily felt something rub up against her leg. She looked down at a very large orange and white striped cat. She gave Andi an amused look.

"It isn't a prerequisite," Andi repeated more forcefully. "It's an option." She grinned at Emily. Andi picked up the hefty feline, who offered no resistance. "Emily, this is Butch. Butch, meet my new friend Emily." She leaned close to the cat and whispered loud enough for Emily to hear, "I think you're going to like her."

"Hi, Butch," Emily said to the cat, rubbing her hand over the animal's head. "What a big boy you are."

"Big girl. Butch is a big girl. She was a very butchy kitten when I got her, very rough and tumble, so I thought the name fit."

Emily raised one eyebrow.

"And how do you know so much about lesbians?" Andi teased.

"Hey, I read. And watch TV. I binge-watched *Orange Is the New Black*."

"So you know about lesbians in prison? I'm pretty sure none of them have cats."

"I figured they just left them home."

Andi deposited the large feline on a chair as they passed through the open living room and into the kitchen. "I thought maybe we would sit on the back deck, seeing as it's such a nice evening," Andi said. She took two beers out of the refrigerator and held one up to Emily for her approval. Emily nodded and reached for a bottle. Andi opened a bag of potato chips and poured them into a glass bowl. She handed the bowl to Emily and went back to the refrigerator, this time pulling out a container of French onion dip.

The late summer evening air was warm on Emily's bare arms as she stepped out onto the deck. Four cushioned chairs surrounded a glass-topped table trimmed with dark green metal. The chairs were starting to show some wear and the green floral print fabric was beginning to fade from the sun. The redwood deck ran the entire length of the house, and a small hot tub sat in the far corner, the padded top locked down securely.

Andi set her beer and the container of dip down on the table. "Have a seat," she said.

Emily plopped down and looked around. The grass was still very green and lush for the beginning of September in central New York. Large ash trees that were beginning to shed their leaves trimmed the property in the back and pine trees lined it on each side, creating a sense of privacy and a feeling of peacefulness. A large flower garden, surrounded by a ring of natural brown stones, sat almost dead center on the big lawn. There wasn't a weed in sight. "What a nice backyard you have," Emily said.

"Thank you." Andi twisted the cap off of her beer and took a sip.

"Your garden reminds me of my mom. She had flowers planted everywhere." So many things made her think of her mother.

"You must miss her a lot." It was more of a statement than a question.

Emily swallowed hard and paused before answering. She needed to rein in the feeling of loss her mother's death left in its wake. "I do." Terribly. "But I'm grateful for the time I did have her in my life."

"That's a great attitude."

Emily took a swig of her beer, feeling the bubbles and cool liquid tickle down her throat. She took the moment to compose herself. "I really do feel that way, but it was a process getting there. I was very angry when she first died. You know—the 'why her, why me, why us' kind of stuff. I felt cheated." Cheated was an understatement. Emily had felt like the rug had been pulled out from under her. She lost her mother, her support, her best friend in an instant.

Andi kept her eyes on Emily as she talked. "So, what helped you get over the anger?"

She wasn't totally over it. But well on her way. "Some of it was the passing of time, but mostly it was Mindy. She helped me get through it. She doesn't quite understand death, I think, but she understands life, and she knows Mom had life and we were lucky that she shared it with us. I'm not explaining it very well. Mindy just kind of has a way of telling you that everything is okay and making you believe it."

"Wow. I thought Mindy was lucky to have you, but it sounds like you are both very lucky to have each other."

"We are. I'm getting to know my sister again. She was still pretty young when I went away to college, and I only saw her when I was home on break. I moved into my own place right after I graduated." Emily felt comfortable around Andi. "Oh, by the way, Mindy and I are having a little get-together next week. Mindy invited one of her friends and I was hoping you could join us."

"Of course. I would love to meet Mindy."

"Excellent." Emily couldn't help but smile. "I seem to be hogging the conversation here. I want to hear more about you."

"No, no, I enjoy your hogging. Go on." Andi smiled broadly. "Hog away."

"No, seriously, your turn. Tell me about your life." Emily truly wanted to know more about Andi, as well as feeling the need to change the subject before she started crying.

"What do you want to know?"

"You grew up with four older brothers. What was that like?"

Andi smiled. "When I was very young, I was the little princess. I could do no wrong. But as I got older and wanted to do stuff with them, hang around them and their friends, they thought of me more as a nuisance, you know? They were doing all the fun things, playing basketball, going to movies, getting into trouble. I wanted to tag along."

"That must have been hard for you." Emily pictured a young Andi, with those beautiful brown eyes, looking forlorn as her brothers trotted off on an adventure without her. The image tugged at Emily's heart, and she had the urge to wrap her arms around the imagined Andi and comfort her.

"It was, for a while. My dad thought that girls shouldn't be doing 'boy' things." Andi made air quotes with her fingers. "And my mother was so overwhelmed trying to raise them and keep them in line and out of trouble that she didn't have a whole lot of time left over for me."

Emily reached over and rubbed Andi's shoulder.

"I spent a lot of time at my grandmother's. She was my escape, a really great lady. She taught me a lot about life, all the important stuff like making chicken soup and how to sew—and I guess, just being myself. She taught me it was okay to be me. She gave me a great sense of self-worth."

"She sounds wonderful. This was your father's mother?"

"Yes, the one I was named after."

"How old were you when she died?" Emily asked.

Emily could see Andi smile through the fading light of day. "Oh, she didn't die. At the age of seventy-nine, she got herself a boyfriend, and they decided to travel around the world. They're in Sicily right now. I'm sure she's over there teaching them all how to cook." Andi laughed.

"Wow, that's great."

"It is. She sends me postcards from wherever they are. They come home every couple of months, but they don't stay home long before they're off globe-trotting again."

"How about the rest of your family? How is your relationship with them now?" Emily asked. "Do they know you're gay?"

"Yeah, they know," Andi said, answering the last question first. "They weren't too happy about it at first. My mother was convinced that it was her fault because she didn't spend enough time with me when I was a kid. She has that classic mother guilt that somehow makes you feel guilty for making her feel guilty." Andi absently ran her finger up the side of her beer bottle to catch a drip before setting it down on the table. "They're all right with it for the most part. I see them from time to time and things are fine. We don't talk about it much. My brothers are all married now with families of their own. I guess God must have thought there were enough boys in our family because every single one of them has only daughters. I have seven nieces."

"I guess they have a lot of little girls tagging along now."

"Poetic justice."

"Does anyone at work know you're gay?" Emily paused. "I hope I'm not getting too personal with the questions."

"Not at all, I don't mind talking about it." She smiled. "With you."

Emily smiled in return. She wasn't sure the warm feeling that was enveloping her was from the conversation and company or from the beer. Either way, she liked it.

"Some people at work know. I don't advertise my sexuality but I don't hide it either. They seem cool with it. I haven't heard any negative remarks from anyone. The students, of course, don't know. At least, as far as I know, they don't."

"I'm glad no one gives you a hard time. I'd have to defend your honor and beat the crap out of them for you."

"You would, would you? Somehow I can't picture you beating anyone up." She laughed.

"Alright, maybe I would just give them a good tongue-lashing." Now that she *could* do for Andi if it was called for. Not that Andi couldn't take care of herself. Emily was sure she could.

"You know Sandra Polly, the French teacher, and Brenda Sherman, one of the gym teachers?" Andi asked.

"I know who they are. I don't know them very well."

Andi paused as if she were choosing her words very carefully. "Well, Sandra used to be married to Robert Martinez, the English teacher. Now she lives with Brenda."

It took a minute for Emily to catch on. "You mean, um…the two women are now together? As a couple?"

"Yep." Andi nodded.

Emily was a bit surprised she hadn't caught on to this when she met the women. She needed to hone her gaydar. "So, at least part of my theory is correct." Emily drank from her bottle waiting for the question, trying not to smirk.

"Okay, I'll bite. What theory?"

"Lesbians and gym teachers. I got it right by fifty percent on that one." The potato chip Andi playfully threw at Emily lodged itself in her hair. Emily laughed and attempted to remove it but only managed to break it into pieces.

"A little help here, Miss Potato Chip Thrower." She pointed to her hair.

"Oops. Shouldn't have done that."

"No worries."

Andi stood up and delicately pulled at strands of Emily's hair as she removed bits of chips. Emily found herself looking at the tanned skin on Andi's neck. Her eyes followed it down until it reached the top swell of her breasts visible at the open collar of her white shirt. Andi's voice pulled her eyes away.

"Okay, all set. Got it." She held several small pieces of potato chips in the palm of her hand and showed the pieces to Emily. "Would you like this back? It still looks fairly edible."

"Um, I'm thinking no."

Andi tossed the pieces over the deck railing onto the lawn.

"That's littering, young lady."

"The squirrels will get it."

"God made junk food for people to eat, not squirrels. You never see a squirrel eating cotton candy, do you? No. God made cotton candy for people. I like to think of it as health food for our souls. If your squirrels gain twenty pounds we'll know why." Emily snickered.

"I'll keep that in mind," Andi said.

There was barely a break in the conversation when Emily asked, "So how come there's no one special in your life?" She gazed into Andi's eyes as she waited for the answer.

"Wow, okay, guess there is no more small talk with you," she said grinning. "Hmm, let's see, I've told you that I ended a four-year relationship about a year ago, and since then, I haven't found anyone that I want to be with."

"I would think you would have to beat the women off with a stick."

"Yes, that is exactly what I've been doing and now no one wants to come near me because there is this ugly rumor going around that I beat women with sticks."

"Okay, you don't have to tell me."

"I'm sorry," Andi said.

Emily didn't think she really was. She seemed to enjoy teasing Emily, and Emily didn't mind it one bit.

"I'm very choosy and don't feel like dating just for the sake of dating. I'm waiting for that special person to love who can love me back. Does that sound corny?"

Emily thought it was very romantic and told Andi as much.

"I think that has been part of the problem. I *am* very romantic. I want the whole package. The love, the commitment, the humor, the intimacy, the sharing. Did I mention the intimacy?"

"As a matter of fact, you did. Was that a problem in your last relationship?" The sun was starting to set and the nearly full moon cast a soft glow on the night and across Andi's silky skin. It didn't escape Emily's notice.

"Emotional intimacy was a problem. I never really felt connected to Janice. That was her name—Janice. I'm pretty sure it still is." Andi joked, then got serious again. "I think I spent most of the four years we were together trying to make it work. Our relationship toward the end went something like this." Andi paused, gathering up her thoughts. "Janice would say or do something thoughtless or mean and I would try to talk to her about it and end up crying. She would feel bad about making me cry and treat me extra nice for a while, but she never addressed the real issue. I would still be hurt or mad and she would get angry all over again because her *nice* tactic wasn't working. I had this image in my mind for a long time of who she was, and the reality was that she was nothing like that. You know what I mean?"

"I do. That sounds a lot like my marriage." Emily took a long swig of her beer and rolled the bottle in her hands.

"You were married?" Andi sounded surprised.

"Yes, for six years. I don't count the last year while we were in the process of getting a divorce. I probably shouldn't count any of it as anything but wasted time."

"That's sad."

"Yes, let's go with that. Let's go with sad. It sounds better than pathetic." Emily knew she must sound bitter. But the truth was, she had almost no emotions surrounding any of it anymore.

"Why pathetic?" Andi leaned forward.

"I guess because I never really loved him, and I married him anyway because it was as close to love as I had gotten. I'll tell you something that I learned from the relationship, though. I know that happiness has to come from within, and another person can't make you happy."

"But they sure as hell can make you miserable."

"Amen to that." Emily raised her beer bottle toward Andi's, clinking them together. She watched as the moonlight danced in Andi's brown eyes. Emily cleared her throat, suddenly at a loss for words. Flustered. She wasn't sure why. She turned her head and stared out into the evening. She found herself relaxing into the silence between them. There was a comfort in it that said more than many actual conversations Emily had had with other people.

Emily spoke at last. "How come you don't have a lot of mosquitoes around here? They would be eating us alive at home by now."

"The bats keep them in check," Andi said.

"Seriously? Bats?" Emily ducked as if avoiding one. Her eyes searched the sky before turning them back to Andi. "Did I happen to mention that I'm afraid of bats?"

"For real? They won't hurt you, Emily. Bats are our friends. Tell you what, if any bat comes near you I'll get my big stick that I use to beat the women off and scare them away."

"Very funny. Okay, I am going to trust you on this. Bats are our friends. Bats are our friends." They both burst out laughing.

When the laughter died down, Emily said, "Okay, no more heavy subjects for the evening. Let's see, what would be a good superficial question? Hmm. Oh, I know. What's your biggest pet peeve?"

Andi thought about her answer for a moment. Tilting her beer bottle toward Emily, she said, "Okay, here's one, I hate it when people use the word *literally* when there is no possible way that what they are saying can be taken literally. For example, if someone says, I *literally* ate a thousand hot dogs this week. Well, they didn't really eat a thousand hot dogs so…you know what I'm saying, right?"

Emily nodded.

"So, how about you? Biggest pet peeve?"

"Bats!"

"Bats, huh? A strange pet peeve. Tell you what, if any bats come near you, I will give them a good tongue-lashing."

"Gee, thanks." Emily said.

Andi suddenly stood and moved her chair closer to Emily. So close, in fact, that when she sat back down Emily could feel a current of electricity between the fraction of an inch of air separating their arms.

"What are you doing?" Emily asked, not minding the closeness at all.

"Protecting you," Andi answered, with straight face but a hint of a tease in her voice.

No, Emily didn't mind the closeness at all.

CHAPTER FIVE

Emily walked around the room checking the progress of her students' drawings as they worked. "Don't pick your pencil up off the paper," she told Kerry. "I want you to do a contour drawing all in one continuous line." The young girl nodded.

The skill level of the class varied greatly. The talent of some was quite obvious, while others struggled with each assignment. Emily noted which of the students would need the most help to get through the class.

She silently walked up behind two boys with their heads together, chatting quietly. She tapped one on the shoulder and then tapped her finger on the drawing. The whispering stopped. The silence in the room was broken by the sound of the bell, indicating the end of the period. Emily was used to the sound by now.

"Everyone, make sure your name is on the back of your paper and put them on my desk, whether you're finished or not." Emily had to raise her voice over the noise of students getting up and chairs scraping against the floor.

One more period to go. The last class was her oil painting class. Because the students had to complete two drawing classes and a color theory class in order to qualify for it, it was her smallest class. It was also Emily's favorite. The students were highly motivated because most of them wanted to continue with art after high school. Oil painting was Emily's personal passion.

"*Miss* Sanders." The stern woman from her first day was back. Emily now knew her name was Rebecca Bowman, the office secretary. She was also known amongst the teachers by several other terms, but Emily refused to join in the name calling.

Emily smiled brightly at her as if the smile would be contagious and force some happiness into the miserable woman. "What can I do for you, Mrs. Bowman?"

"Your sister called and left you a message."

"Is everything okay?" *Why would Mindy be calling the school office?* Emily had given her that number for emergencies only.

"She said to remind you to pick up bread for supper. Apparently, your cell phone is turned off. In the future, I wish you would inform your sister and anyone else, for that matter, that the school office is not your personal answering service." She turned and was gone before Emily had the chance to thank her.

Emily shook her head. Bringing bread home for dinner was definitely not an emergency. Emily would have to talk to her about that.

Mindy had been excited all week. They were having what she called a "party dinner." Emily didn't consider having one of Mindy's many *best friends* and Andi over for dinner to be a party. But if Mindy wanted to call it that and treat it like an "event," Emily didn't mind. Calling the school for bread was another story.

Emily was still deep in thought when her final class of the day began to shuffle into the room. The students went directly to the shelves in the back of the room and retrieved their boxes of supplies. "Class, set up at your easels and let's get started. Charlie, can you turn on the lights for the still life setup? And throw out your gum." The room grew quiet. Emily turned on the radio, set to the local soft rock station. It was a habit she had gotten into when she painted in college. It relaxed her and she thought it helped the kids the same way it did for her. She kept the volume low as she walked from student to student giving personal instruction and pointers where she felt the young artists needed help.

After the last of the students left her classroom for the day, Emily grabbed her coat and backpack, locked the door, and headed in the direction of Andi's classroom.

❖

Andi looked up from the papers she was grading, saw Emily, and couldn't help but smile. "Well, hello there."

"Hi yourself," Emily replied, with a smile of her own. "I wanted to make sure you were all set on directions to my house." She leaned her hip against the corner of Andi's desk.

Andi didn't fail to notice the creamy skin that peeked through the gap at Emily's waist as her shirt pulled up with the movement. She forced her eyes upward to answer the question.

"I am. Straight down Freemont, take a left onto Taft, right onto Church Street to Rose Terrace. Your address is already programed into my GPS just in case. I'm really looking forward to this evening and meeting Mindy." *And spending time with you,* she thought but didn't say out loud.

"Dinner is at six thirty, but feel free to come by earlier if you want to."

"I thought I would bring wine. Is Chardonnay okay?"

"Perfect. I better get going," Emily said. "I have to stop at the grocery store before I go home. I'll see you soon."

Andi watched her walk out the door, shook her head at the fact that she'd done that, and went back to grading her papers. She finished in time to run home, change into jeans, and be at Emily's house a little after six.

"You must be Mindy," Andi said to the young lady who opened the door for her. Emily stuck her head out of the kitchen in time to see Andi give Mindy a big hug. "Emily has told me so much about you that I feel like I already know you."

They were still hugging when Emily came up behind them. Andi reached around Mindy and handed Emily a bottle of wine.

"Mindy, you have to let her go so she can come in," Emily said.

Mindy let Andi go. "Hello, Andi. It so nice to meet you," Mindy said, grabbing Andi's hand.

"Nice to meet you too." Mindy pumped her hand up and down. Andi laughed and turned to Emily. "Hi there."

"I see you found it okay. Come on in, and I'll show you around." Emily had also changed out of her work clothes into faded jeans and sweater. Andi liked the casual look on her. Emily handed Mindy the wine. "Can you put this in the fridge, honey?"

Much to Andi's surprise, Emily took her hand and led her down a short hallway. Andi avoided the desire to intertwine their fingers and chastised herself for even thinking it. Dropping Andi's hand as suddenly as she had grabbed it, Emily raised her arms in the air and said in an imitation spokesmodel voice, "And here we have the living room." She waved her hands about. "This room was the reason I fell in love with the house."

Andi could see why. It was cozy, with enough room for the oversized brown couch and a matching recliner chair, both of which were positioned to get the best view of the large flat-screen TV that sat on the library table against the wall. An array of bowls and plates filled with chips, crackers, and cheeses sat on the solid oak coffee table in front of the couch. Emily had obviously gone to a lot of work. "Very nice," Andi said, bringing her eyes up to Emily's.

"Actually, it was this little cove over here that first caught my eye," Emily said, leading Andi to the right. The small room held a stone fireplace with a thick wood mantel and a beautiful bay window that looked out over a private backyard. A love seat anchored the space, with the same brown fabric as the couch, and a hand-woven earth-tone rug lay on the floor. A generous stack of wood sat at the ready in the fireplace and more wood was neatly piled on the wrought iron rack off to the side.

"Very cozy." Andi said, looking around. *Very cozy and very romantic.* "Great place." Her eyes stopped on the paintings hanging on the far wall. "Oh my God. Are these yours?" Andi looked at Emily, impressed.

Emily nodded.

"These are incredible." Andi returned her attention to the art. She took her time as she scanned each one. "Oil paintings, right?"

"Yes."

Andi studied the landscape painting directly in front of her. "I love this one. It has a sensuality about it that I've only seen in figure paintings, never a landscape. The gentle rolling of the meadow and curves of the land remind me of a female body." Andi regretted the statement as soon as it was out of her mouth. What would Emily think with her comparing it to a naked woman? Andi kept her eyes on the art searching for better words to describe it. The scene was right before sunset, the trees alive with the color of fire. "It seems to glow from within. I like them all, but this one is my favorite," Andi said, at last, pulling her eyes from it to look at Emily.

"Thank you," Emily said, seemingly shy all of a sudden.

"No, Em, I mean it. It's like I can see your soul in these paintings."

Emily blushed. "Come on, I'll show you my studio."

Andi was equally impressed with the painting that sat on the easel in the studio. It wasn't done yet, but it was well on its way. Some of what Andi assumed was the underpainting was done in reddish brown, and bits of it still showed through the colors that Emily had applied over the top of it.

"This room was perfect for my studio because of that big window. It faces south and lets sunlight in even this late in the day."

Andi nodded, noticing a drawing on the table in the corner. It was just a rough sketch of the backside of a nude female. "Did you use a model for this?" Andi asked, actually hoping the answer was no. She wasn't sure why.

"Oh no. It's just from my head. Although if I had been, it more than likely would have been done by now. I've been working on it on and off for months. I can't seem to get it just right."

"I think it's great. When do you have time to work on your own art?" Andi asked.

"Mostly late at night. It's like meditation for me. It helps me sleep."

"So, is that why you create art? Because it helps you relax?"

"I have so many ideas in my head that I need to get out. I guess I paint so I don't go insane. Better to be an artist than a mass murderer, I always say."

"Good point." Andi chuckled.

"Can I show Andi my room?" Mindy asked, as she bounced in. Emily looked at Andi and raised her eyebrows, silently giving Andi the choice.

"Of course you can." Andi linked her arm in Mindy's and was practically dragged out of the studio. Andi gave Emily a quick smile over her shoulder as she was pulled away. "I'll be back," Andi said, giving her best Arnold Schwarzenegger impersonation.

❖

Emily went to check on the progress of the chicken cordon bleu in the oven. The chicken was starting to brown, and so far, the cheese was staying inside and not leaking out onto the pan. *Looking good.* She opened the refrigerator and retrieved the bottle of the wine that Andi brought. *Kendall-Jackson, an excellent choice. I wouldn't expect anything less from that lovely woman.* Emily smiled to herself. She put the bottle on the table and looked through the silverware drawer for her corkscrew. *I should invest in a better one of these*, she thought as she found the old, beat-up tool.

She was struggling to get the cork out of the bottle when Mindy and Andi appeared in the doorway. "Let me help you with that," Andi said. She pulled the cork out smoothly and effortlessly and held it up for Emily to see with a smile of triumph on her face.

"My hero."

Andi gave a playful bow. "Wow, something smells great."

The doorbell rang. "I'll get it," Mindy said, a little too loudly. She ran to the door, leaving Emily and Andi alone in the kitchen.

Andi leaned toward Emily and said in a low voice, "Mindy said I was her best friend."

The closeness of Andi sent a shiver down Emily's spine, startling her. Emily laughed out loud, both at her surprise and at Andi's statement. "I hate to burst your bubble, Andi, but Mindy's other best friends include Daisy—who that should be at the door, Reba McEntire, Rachel from *Friends,* and the entire cast of *Glee.*"

Andi rolled her eyes. "Holy cow! I think I could compete with Reba and Rachel, but I don't stand a chance against the cast of *Glee.* Those kids are good!" She let out a chuckle.

"You got that right. Come on, let's go meet her *other* best friend, Daisy." Andi set the bottle of wine down on the table and followed Emily to the front door. It was going to be a fun evening.

❖

"Oh my, this pie is good." Andi licked the last bit from her fork. "Here you go," she said offering the fork to Emily, grinning ear to ear. "No need to wash this one."

"Okay, I won't. I do that too. I lick the fork clean and put it back in the drawer. In fact, I probably did just that the last time I used that very fork."

Andi laughed. Mindy and Daisy joined in. Emily tried hard

not to laugh at her own joke but couldn't help it, and it came out more like a snort, which started everyone laughing all over again.

"Why don't you girls clear the table and I'll load the dishwasher," Emily said, after the laughter died down.

Andi scraped the dishes into the trash and handed them to Emily. Emily liked having Andi around, and the chore went fast as they chitchatted away.

They were finishing up when the doorbell rang. "My mom's here! My mom's here!" Daisy said, bouncing up and down and clapping her hands. She and Mindy ran to the door, followed closely by Emily. Andi stayed behind to put the last of the silverware in the dishwasher.

"Daisy is a complete doll," Emily told Daisy's mother at the door. "She's welcome here anytime."

There were hugs all around and Andi appeared in time for her goodbye hug from Daisy.

"You have a very nice friend there," Emily said to Mindy as she closed the door.

"She's my *best* friend," Mindy said, to no one in particular.

Emily looked at Andi and winked. *I've got a very nice friend as well.*

"Well, Mindy, what do you say you go get ready for bed? Remember we have to get an early start in the morning. Get some sleep." Emily tapped her sister gently on the shoulder, careful not to sound too bossy. She was still learning how to tread around Mindy.

"Yeah. We gonna go visit my daddy tomorrow," Mindy said to Andi.

"I know, Emily told me. I hope you have a great visit."

"Okay," was her simple answer. She turned to go, but stopped abruptly, grabbed Andi, and pulled her into a hug. "V-v-very nice meeting you, Andi."

"You too, sweetie."

Mindy turned and disappeared down the hall.

Emily smiled at Andi. The evening couldn't have gone better

and Andi was so good with Mindy. Emily's heart swelled, and she actually felt her eyes tearing up. She cleared her throat. "How about another glass of wine and then we can watch a movie?" Emily offered, hoping Andi would stay.

"Are you sure? I know you have to get up early tomorrow too."

I'm very sure. "Absolutely. Sit, make yourself comfortable, and I'll be right back."

Emily came back with two glasses of wine, handed one to Andi, then sat next to her on the couch. She picked up the remote and hit the button for Netflix.

"How about *Jerry Maguire?*" Emily asked. "An oldie, but a goody."

"Sure. I've never seen it before."

Emily started the movie and let out an audible sigh as she leaned back into the soft cushions of the couch and pulled her bare feet up next to her. She sipped her wine. "I can't believe you've never seen this."

"Believe it," Andi said. "I never lie about movies I haven't seen. Besides, I usually only watch movies that have girl-on-girl action."

Emily gave her a playful slap, her curiosity piqued by the thought of what a girl-on-girl movie would be like.

"Hey! I almost spilled my wine. That would be alcohol abuse," Andi said.

"Shh, the movie's starting," Emily said, with a smile.

Andi and Emily made comments here and there as the movie played but watched most of it in comfortable silence.

As the movie was nearing the end, Emily stretched her legs out in front of her, trying to get more comfortable. "Put your feet up here," Andi said, patting her lap. "I'll give you a foot massage."

Emily took only a moment to respond. She shifted her position on the couch, gently placing both feet in Andi's lap and leaned back comfortably against the arm of the couch. Her attention returned to the movie as Andi's fingers worked expertly on her foot starting with just enough pressure right below the toes. As the stress left Emily's body, a new sensation moved in. The tingling that started in her foot quickly moved up her leg and settled momentarily in the pit of her stomach, before moving down again and causing a stir and surge of moisture. *Wow. What the hell?* She tried to justify the feelings and her body's response to it. *I've just been lonely and I'm enjoying the attention, that's all.* She willed her body to stop its response to Andi's touch.

"You complete me," Tom said to Renée in the movie.

"She doesn't want to complete you," Andi said to the television. "She wants you to come to her *already* whole and complete."

Emily was immediately pulled out of her own thoughts. She looked at Andi and raised her eyebrows.

"Did I say that out loud?" Andi scrunched up her face.

Emily couldn't hold back her smile and they both burst out laughing. Emily gave her a playful kick.

They brought their attention back to the television screen and Andi once again moved her strong hands over Emily's feet. The sensations throughout Emily's body returned. Confused, she quickly pulled her feet away and sat up. "It's tickling me," she lied, betrayed by her body's reaction. She wasn't just moist— she hated that word. She was downright wet. It scared her. How could Andi touching her *feet* make her wet? Make her tingle? It made no sense. The urge to move farther away from Andi was matched by her desire to move closer. She ignored both. When she dared to glance at Andi she saw a look of disappointment that Andi almost managed to cover with a smile.

"Sorry," Andi started.

"No, I'm sorry," Emily interrupted. "I have sensitive feet." Another lie. But she couldn't admit the truth. She didn't even know what the truth was.

They finished watching the movie in silence.

Andi rose as the credits played. "Thank you so much for inviting me over. I had a great time."

"Me too," Emily said honestly. "I truly enjoyed your company. We'll have to do this again soon." They exchanged a quick hug at the door and Andi was gone. Emily felt weirdly alone.

Emily turned off the television, brought the wineglasses into the kitchen, shut off lights, and made her way to the bathroom. "What the heck is wrong with you?" she said to her reflection in the mirror. She brushed her teeth, changed into her nightgown, and climbed into bed. She lay awake, unable to sleep as her mind replayed the events of the evening and the sensations that coursed through her body at Andi's touch. She didn't know what to make of it. She tried to justify it to herself. She hadn't had sex or even had someone touch her in a very long time. That was it. It had to be. There was no way it could be anything else. Or could it?

CHAPTER SIX

Emily put her hand over her mouth to cover a yawn. The lack of sleep from the night before was taking its toll. She pulled into a parking space at Tops grocery store and made a mental note to grab a bottle of Coke along with Mindy's snacks for the hour and a half drive to Rochester.

The sun from the rapidly warming day felt good as it poured in through the car windows. It looked like it would be a very pleasant drive, and a great day to attend the Clothesline Arts Festival.

Emily's hand froze on the door handle when she spotted someone familiar in the passenger seat of a blue Chevy several aisles away. Was that...? Yes, it was Andi. Emily smiled—until the woman sitting in the driver seat leaned over and kissed Andi full on the mouth.

Emily's smile turned into a frown and then into a grimace.

"What's the matter?" Mindy asked her.

"Huh? Why?"

"Your lips are going crazy all over your face."

Emily forced a smile despite the hurt and confusion she felt. *Hurt? Why should I feel hurt? Why am I feeling anything at all? So someone is kissing Andi. Why should I care? What the heck is wrong with me?* Emily backed out of the parking spot without getting out of the car.

"Hey, we didn't get snacks, and you promised," Mindy said.

Emily turned her car away from Andi and the woman and sped out of the parking lot.

"Emily!" Mindy protested.

"We'll stop on the Thruway and get something to eat." She struggled to keep her voice even, still not sure why she was so upset. "Okay, honey?"

Mindy shook her head, obviously not pleased. "Oh, all right, but do not forget."

"Okay, okay," Emily said, a little more curtly than she intended.

Emily spent almost the entire drive wondering what the hell was wrong with her. Her feelings left her confused. Was she jealous? *Jealous of what?* Andi certainly had the right to kiss whomever she wanted—and who wouldn't want to kiss Andi, right? Her thoughts went back to the night before and her body's reaction to Andi rubbing her feet. *Knock it off,* she told her brain. But it refused to listen. The barrage continued until she reached the neighborhood she'd grown up in.

She pushed the thoughts of Andi and her own reactions aside as she drove down the familiar street and pulled into her father's driveway. She sat for a minute looking at the place she had grown up in. The large white house was in need of fresh paint, and a shutter on the second floor needed repair. She didn't like the feeling of the house since her mother's death. The warmth was gone. It was just a house now, no longer a home, no longer *her* home.

The lawn had recently been mowed. The long clippings suggested that it had been quite a while between cuttings, and Emily suspected that it had been mowed in anticipation of their arrival. Several birds flew to the bird feeder that hung from the large maple tree in the front yard but flew away again when they discovered there were no seeds to be had. *Mom loved sitting on the porch watching the birds at that feeder.* Emily shook her head. *She would never have let it run empty*. That was how the house seemed to her now. Even from the outside, it felt empty.

"Come on, Emily," Mindy said. The excited edge to her voice made Emily smile despite the feelings of melancholy. Emily slid out of the car and grabbed the suitcases from the back seat. She handed one to Mindy and had to walk fast to keep up with her as she bounced up the front steps to the porch. Emily wasn't sure if she should knock first or go right in. It was never even a question when her mother was alive. She knew the door was always open to her. Mindy didn't hesitate, but when she turned the doorknob it was locked. She looked confused like she wasn't sure what to do next.

Emily raised her hand to knock but the door was opened from the inside. William Sanders stood in the doorway, arms wide to welcome his daughters. He pulled them both into a big bear hug.

"Come on in, girls," he said with a smile.

The house was dark, despite the lights being on. The curtains were closed tight against the bright sun. Dampness permeated the air. The grandfather clock in the foyer had a layer of dust covering it. It stood silent. It probably hadn't been wound in months. The pendulum stood at attention, motionless. The clock seemed to represent the feeling that surrounded them, still and lifeless.

"How are you, Dad?" Emily asked. They made their way into the living room and set their suitcases down.

"I'm doing okay, kiddo." His reply was less than convincing.

"Would it be all right if I opened the drapes and let some light in here?"

"Sure thing, anything you want." He attempted a smile.

Mindy gave him a big hug. "I miss you soooo much, Daddy."

"I miss you too, baby. How's Emily treating you?"

"Emily is the bestest sister ever."

"I know she is." He bent down and gave Mindy a kiss on the cheek.

She rubbed her skin. "Ow! Daddy, your whiskers are rough."

He ran his hand over his face. "I know. I need a good shave. Let's get these suitcases upstairs so you guys can settle in." He headed up the stairs, both suitcases in hand.

Mindy and Emily started up after him, but Emily stopped. Something on the bookcase by the stairs caught her eye. Emily picked up a large coin and realized it was a one month chip from Alcoholics Anonymous. Under the chip sat a printed schedule for meetings, some of the dates circled. Emily replaced the chip and hurried up after them.

An hour later, after making a late breakfast for her dad and Mindy, Emily pointed her car in the direction of Route 490 and stepped on the gas. Traffic on the expressway was much lighter than it would have been on a workday morning. As she exited onto Goodman Street, Emily began to relax. She looked forward to attending the Clothesline Art Festival every year, and this year would be no exception. It didn't bother her that she was going by herself. It just meant that she could take her time while she checked out the booths of handmade jewelry, paintings, photography, and various other high-end works of art. The Clothesline Festival was one of the best art and craft shows in western New York. Being a highly juried show, the artists who were accepted to show their wares were the best of the best. Emily thought she might even purchase a piece of art for her new home if anything spoke to her.

She found a parking spot right on Goodman Street, a short walk away from the festival. Her parallel parking skills were put to the test as she maneuvered her car into the tight space, but she pulled it off with no problem.

A sigh escaped her lips as she felt the fresh warm air that indicated the final days of summer, and her walk was light and confident as she traveled the two blocks to the festival. She was in her element now. This was the area she grew up in, and she was about to mingle with other artists. Yes, this was her comfort zone. She paid her five-dollar admission fee and entered the outdoor show.

Pausing briefly inside the entrance, Emily could hear the kettle corn calling her name. She answered the call and purchased a small bag, nibbling away as she started her trek around the grounds. She walked past several booths of stained glass, abstract paintings, and portrait photography, stopping at a jewelry booth to look at a pair of earrings that caught her eye. The delicate silver wire gently cradled a small tiger-eye stone that hung from a silver stud post. She held them up to her ears and checked herself in a small mirror that hung from the side of the display. *They don't work with the color of my eyes. But they would look great with Andi's brown eyes.* She felt a pang in her chest. Andi. Andi who was being kissed very intimately by a woman. *For God's sake, knock it off,* she reprimanded herself silently. She replaced the earrings on the rack and did her best to push the image from her mind.

Once again, she focused her attention on the artwork surrounding her. She strolled leisurely, stopping here and there, chatting with various artists. As she was leaving a booth of local photographs, she ran smack into Lauren Burns, literally. Lauren lived across the street from her parents' house—well, her dad's house now. "So sorry. Oh my God, Lauren. How are you?" she asked, trying to compose herself.

Lauren leaned in for a hug. "I'm doing great. How's your new job? How are you doing in Syracuse? How's Mindy?"

"I really like it there. The school is great. The kids are great. Mindy's adjusting well."

"I'm glad," Lauren said. Emily could hear the sincerity in her voice. "So, how is your dad doing? I wave to him every once in a while, when I see him outside, but that isn't too often."

"He's trying." She didn't go into detail. "So, what're you doing here? Looking for art to purchase?"

Lauren brushed a strand of her honey blond hair out of her

face. "I am helping my sister. She does watercolor. Her booth is down there." She pointed down the aisle several booths ahead. "I don't think you've ever met her."

"I don't think so either, but I would love to see her work."

"Come on then." Lauren linked her arm in Emily's and led the way to the booth.

Emily looked around at the large paintings that hung inside the white tent. Impressive. The use of colors and negative space, as well as the use of light and shadows, brought this art up to a whole different level than most of the art she had seen here today.

As soon as the artist finished talking to a potential buyer, she turned her attention to her sister and Emily. Emily noticed the family resemblance immediately. Both sisters had very straight honey blond hair, although Lauren's was much longer, green eyes with thick, blond lashes. Both women were beautiful. The artist's quick smile made her appear even more so. She looked to be a few years older than Lauren, which would make her somewhat older than Emily as well.

"Sarah, this is my friend Emily. Emily, Sarah. Emily's dad has the white house across from me."

"Hello," Emily said, holding out her hand.

"So nice to meet you." Sarah's hand was soft, but her handshake firm. She continued to hold Emily's hand while talking. "I think I've seen you before when I was at Lauren's."

Emily searched her memory. *I think I would have noticed meeting someone as hot as you. Oh my God, what is up with me noticing how good women look lately?*

"We didn't actually meet," Sarah continued. "I noticed you from across the street."

How can anyone have teeth that white and perfect? Emily realized she was looking a little too intensely at Sarah's mouth. She looked down at the ground in an attempt to hide her blush and the grin she was trying to suppress. When she looked up at Sarah again, Emily found herself captured by deep green eyes.

"As I recall, Lauren told me you're an art teacher."

Her hand was still in Sarah's, and Emily was surprised that the contact wasn't making her uncomfortable in the least. "Yes. I teach in Syracuse now." She was staring again.

Lauren's voice broke the trace she was in. "Sarah, I need to get going. I have to pick Sean up from his friend's house." Sean, Lauren's ten-year-old son, had often done odd jobs for Emily's mother. "Anything you want me to do before I go?"

"No, I think I am all set here. Thanks so much for helping me this morning. I really appreciate it." Sarah let go of Emily's hand so she could give her sister a hug.

"It was so nice to see you, Lauren. Mindy and I are at Dad's all weekend if you want to stop over," Emily told her.

Lauren reached over and gave Emily's shoulder a squeeze. "Great to see you too. Maybe I'll see you later." With that, she turned and left.

The two women watched her walk away for a moment and then turned back toward each other.

"So, do you like teaching?" Sarah continued the conversation.

"I love it. I have a steady job and I get to do my own art on the side. It's a win-win situation."

"I can understand that. It is very difficult making a living with just your artwork these days. I do all right, but I wouldn't mind doing a little better." Sarah smiled broadly.

"Your work is wonderful." Emily broke the intense eye contact to glance at the paintings lining the walls of the booth. "You have quite an eye for beauty." Emily felt like she could reach out and touch the petals on a painting of an orchid and actually feel their velvety texture.

"I sure do," Sarah replied, her eyes never leaving Emily.

She's flirting with me.

Is she flirting with me?

I think she's flirting with me.

The nervous feeling in the pit of Emily's stomach was a familiar one. *Okay, enough of this shit*, she told herself. *So what if she's flirting with me? I don't need to get all nervous about it.*

So what? A beautiful woman is flirting with me. She certainly is beautiful, isn't she? Emily smiled at Sarah despite her thoughts. Or maybe she smiled because of her thoughts.

"Tell me about your art." Sarah's smile matched Emily's.

"Excuse me. Can you tell me the price of this painting?" Neither woman noticed an older gentleman who had entered the booth.

"I am going to let you get back to work," Emily said. Time to bow out of this situation. Besides, it wasn't fair of her to take Sarah's time while she was working.

"I'll be with you in one second." Sarah held up one finger to the man. She took one of her business cards from the table at the front of the booth and handed it to Emily. "Have a drink with me later. It would be fun, and I would love to hear more about your art." Her fingers brushed Emily's hand as Emily accepted the card. An unexpected tingle traveled through Emily, startling her.

"Call me after six thirty. I'll be done here by then." Sarah turned her attention back to the man who had asked the question.

Emily tucked the card into the front pocket of her jeans. Flattered by the attention, she doubted she would take Sarah up on the offer. Would it be rude not to call? She slipped quietly out of the booth.

The next several booths held no interest, and Emily passed them by with barely a glance. Farther down, a charcoal drawing caught her eye. She stepped inside the tent to take a better look. It was a drawing of a female. The figure was sitting with her back to the viewer with one hip perched on a stool. The model's dark hair and the side of her face, barely visible, reminded Emily of Andi. Again, the image of Andi kissing someone came to the forefront of her mind, causing a pang in her heart. She ran her fingers over the business card in her pocket and forced her thoughts from Andi to Sarah. Maybe she would call her after all.

❖

EMILY'S ART AND SOUL

"So tell me about your new chick," Taylor said to Andi before they had even sat down with their food.

Andi shook her head and slid into the booth. They'd known each other since college, but Taylor's choice of words sometimes still made Andi take pause. "She is not my *new chick*."

"You said you like her." Taylor stabbed a French fry with her plastic fork and moved it to her mouth, waiting for an answer.

"As a friend. I like her as a friend. She's straight. And she's been through an awful lot the last year or so. The last thing she needs is some lesbian making moves on her."

Taylor chuckled. "You are not just *some* lesbian. You are a lesbian *extraordinaire*." She stuffed the French fry in her mouth.

"True," Andi said. "But, not going to happen." There was no way she would ever make moves on Emily. She wanted to keep her *in* her life, not send her running. She unwrapped her cheeseburger and lifted the top bun, assessing the amount of ketchup and mustard. Satisfied, she took a bite. She enjoyed her outings with Taylor, but Taylor seemed hell-bent on Andi finding a new love interest. It wasn't that Andi was against the idea. She just needed to find a *lesbian*, not some straight woman, no matter how attractive and interesting and funny said straight woman was. She consciously pushed thoughts of Emily aside and turned her attention back to Taylor. "What about you? Any new *chicks* in your life?" Andi asked, purposely using Taylor's word.

"As a matter of fact…" Taylor opened her hazel eyes wide.

Andi was envious of those thick dark lashes, in total contrast to her red hair.

"Nope. No new chicks in my life."

"I love how dramatic you are."

"Drama is my middle name, darling." Taylor waved her hand through the air in small circles and tossed her long hair over her shoulder. "Actually, that's not true. My middle name is Gertrude."

Andi laughed. "You are such a liar. Your middle name is Marie."

"But Gertrude is so much less mundane. So, seriously, tell me about your new friend," she said, using air quotes with the word *friend*.

Andi let out an exasperated breath. She knew Taylor was teasing, but Andi did need to keep Emily in the friend category for real, and Taylor wasn't helping. She proceeded to tell her about Emily, leaving out the parts about how pretty she found her and how her beautiful blue eyes lit up when she smiled.

"I'm not convinced," Taylor said, when Andi finished.

"Of what?"

"That she's in the friend zone for you."

Andi shook her head. But the truth was, she wasn't convinced of that either.

CHAPTER SEVEN

What am I doing? Emily asked herself. She punched in the number on the business card and put her phone up to her ear. *Maybe she won't answer. I hope she doesn't answer. I think...*

"Hello," Sarah answered.

"Um, hi."

"Emily? Hi. I was hoping you would call."

"Um, yeah?" *Oh my God, could you sound like more of an idiot?* "Hi, yes. Well, I thought maybe I would take you up on that drink offer. I mean if the offer is still good. I know you must be tired and all."

"Absolutely, the offer is still good. How does eight thirty sound? There's a great place in Pittsford. Rumors. Have you heard of it?"

"It's in Schoen Place, right?" Emily asked.

Emily could hear a muffled sound on the other end of the line as she heard Sarah ask someone else. "It's in Schoen Place, right?" Emily wasn't sure but she thought a male voice said, "Yes."

"Sorry, yes, that's the place. Is that all right? Should I meet you there or would you like me to pick you up?"

Emily still wasn't sure what she was doing. Was a new friend asking her to have a drink or was she being asked out on a date? She suspected it was the latter. She had never done anything like this before. Just the thought of it made her nervous.

But there was something intriguing about it all too. She'd never had a woman ask her out on a date before and was flattered by the attention. Whereas she'd never been fond of attention from men. *Hmm. Wonder why? This probably isn't a date. I'm making myself crazy. She's a nice person asking me to have a drink.* Emily had the urge to call Andi and talk to her about it. No. She wasn't going to call Andi. She was fully capable of making a decision about this on her own.

"Emily?"

"Um, yes, I'm here." She had to think back to the question. "Yes, that's fine. I can meet you there. You said eight thirty, right?" *Okay, guess I made a decision.*

"Yes. Super. I'll see you there."

Emily hit the End button on her iPhone and closed her fist around it. "I hope you know what you're doing," she said to herself. *Of course, I don't. Oh my God, what am I going to wear?*

❖

Emily pulled into a parking space, lucky to find a spot so close to Rumors in the lot shared by a number of small shops and restaurants. She took a deep breath and fought off the feeling of nausea creeping from her stomach up her throat. Stepping out of the car, she pulled her wallet from her backpack and threw her backpack on the back seat, slipping the wallet into the rear pocket of her dark denim jeans. Another deep breath.

She tugged her deep pink cable knit sweater down in the back and straightened the simple gold chain around her neck. Both bought on sale from J.Jill. She ran a hand over her hair to smooth it down. *Nothing to be nervous about. This is most likely just a drink with a new friend...or not.*

"Emily." She turned at the sound of her name. Sarah stopped about a foot and a half away. Her eyes traveled down the length of Emily's body and back up to her eyes. "You look great," she said, with a smile. She stepped closer and gave Emily a hug.

I think this is a date, Emily's brain screamed. She pushed the panic back down her throat with a hard swallow. *Okay, I can handle this. What's so bad about a date with a beautiful woman? And she is beautiful, isn't she? I can handle this. I don't know if I can handle this.* She managed a smile as they walked in.

"Table for two?" the young hostess asked.

"We would like to be seated at the bar if that's all right." Sarah looked at Emily.

Emily nodded. They were led through the restaurant area and up a few steps to the bar in the back.

"What would you like to drink, Emily?" Sarah asked once they were seated.

"A glass of Chardonnay would be great." Chardonnay. That's what Andi brought last night. Andi. Sarah. She was with Sarah, shouldn't be thinking about Andi.

Sarah flagged the bartender. His quick smile lit up his handsome face. The top two buttons of his neatly pressed white shirt were undone, a hint of soft chest hair visible. His jeans were a bit too tight. Emily glanced at him briefly, then looked past him at the large mirror behind the bar. She saw herself sitting next to a very beautiful woman. *This looks right.* The thought surprised her.

"Can we get two glasses of Chardonnay? Your best," Sarah said.

Emily turned her gaze from the mirror to look at Sarah directly, her smile genuine. She was going to enjoy this evening and enjoy the company of this woman. The number of butterflies in her stomach seemed to lessen, and the alcohol would take care of any of the little critters that remained. They made small talk until the wine arrived.

"I'm so glad you agreed to meet me. I'm sure your time must be limited on your visit."

"I'm so glad you asked me." In this moment, Emily meant it, and she found herself relaxing into the conversation.

"So, Emily, you've seen my art. Tell me about yours."

Emily liked the way her name sounded when Sarah said it, deep and rich. "I work mostly in oils. I love landscapes, especially early morning or evening scenes, the way the sun dances on the trees as it sets or rises."

Sarah nodded and reached for her drink. Emily did the same. "Do you work from photos or plein air?" Sarah asked, using the French term meaning "in the open air." Sarah sipped her wine, but her eyes never left Emily.

"I take photos whenever I get the chance. I work mostly from those. I don't get a chance to paint outside too often."

"I can understand that," Sarah said. She ran her hand through her blond hair. Emily noticed that it had a light curl to it that wasn't there earlier. She had also changed her clothes and had applied more makeup. Her gray slacks were slimming and her dark blue blouse showed a hint of cleavage, which Emily noticed but did her best not to let her eyes linger on. She wore no jewelry other than the diamond studs in her pierced ears.

"I also have my school schedule to work around and my younger sister, Mindy. She came to live with me recently. So it's easier to work from photos. But I try to get outside to watch sunrises and sunsets whenever possible, to sort of take mental notes for future paintings."

"Very nice. Do you have pictures of your work?"

"As a matter of fact, I do." Emily pulled her iPhone out of her pocket, opened her photos, and clicked on the *Artwork* album. She brought up the first picture and handed the phone to Sarah.

"Wow. Nice."

"Thanks," Emily said. She studied Sarah as Sarah studied the art on her phone. Thin nose with a tiny, barely noticeable freckles, perfectly groomed eyebrows darker than her blond hair, full red lips. Lips.

Sarah looked up. If she knew Emily had been staring, she didn't say anything. Instead she said, "These last two are different from the rest. A whole different style. These are yours too?" She flipped the phone around to show Emily what she was talking about.

The pieces *were* different, somewhat of an experiment. An attempt at stepping out of her comfort zone. Emily gave up the experiment and went back to what she knew. She wasn't much of a risk taker. "They're mine. I was just messing with some pastels. Nothing serious." She brought her attention to her glass of wine, swirling the liquid around before taking a sip. Actually it was more like a gulp. What was she doing?

Sarah continued. "I like them. I can see that you are more comfortable with the landscapes, though. But it never hurts to try something new. I've always had trouble painting landscapes. I stick to flowers and still life because I feel like I have more control over them."

"So, you're a woman who likes to be in control?" Emily asked. *Oh my God, why did I say that? I sound like I'm flirting.*

"Oh yes." Sarah raised her eyebrows suggestively. "The only thing I don't have control over is my bladder. I think I need to go to the little girls' room."

"I'll wait here." Emily smiled as she watched Sarah walk away. She was surprised at what a nice time she was having. The nerves had dissipated. Sarah was easy to talk to. That helped. *What would Andi think if she knew I was out on a date with a woman? At least I think I am.* She still didn't know for sure.

"Has anyone ever told you how beautiful you are?" It was the bartender. "On the house," he said, setting another glass of wine on the bar in front of her. "I don't mean to be forward here, but I would love to take you out to dinner sometime." His smile was charming, but Emily had no interest in his offer.

"No, thank you," she said sweetly, sliding the drink back toward him.

He produced a business card from behind the bar, turned it over, and wrote on it. "My cell, in case you change your mind." His smile seemed sincere as he placed the card in her hand.

"And the drink is no strings attached." He held up his hands in surrender as he backed away.

Sarah slid back into her seat and nodded at the new drink in front of Emily. "Starting round two without me?"

"A gift from the bartender," Emily said. Was it okay to let your date know someone else hit on you? She wasn't sure of the rules here.

Almost as if on cue, he returned with another glass of wine and set it in front of Sarah. "Also on the house, for the other beautiful lady," he said with a wink, and walked away.

"Hmm," Sarah said.

"He's right about one thing. You are beautiful." Emily said, shocking herself.

"I was thinking that very same thing about you."

Emily could feel heat rising from her center. Hmm, the bartender made a pass at her and she felt nothing. Sarah complimented her and her body reacted. What? She took another a gulp of wine. "Um, so, how long have you been painting?"

"Just about all my life. My mom likes to tell people I was born with a paintbrush in my hand."

"Ouch," Emily teased. "That must have made your birth even more painful for your mother."

Sarah laughed. "I started taking drawing lessons when I was about seven. I guess my parents got tired of the crayon wall murals and decided to try to channel my artistic talents."

"Did you enjoy the lessons?" Art seemed like a safe subject, and Emily was truly interested. She didn't have any other artists in her circle of friends.

"At first I hated them. I've never been one to play by the rules, and confining my art to one piece of paper didn't seem right. But it did give me the basic skills I needed when I decided I wanted to pursue watercolor."

"And why watercolor?" Emily finished her first drink and set the empty glass on the bar. It only took a few moments for her to reach for her second.

"Watercolor is so free and flowing. It has no boundaries unless *I* decide to put them in. If I am doing a flower, for example, one petal can flow right into the next or it can be totally separate. It becomes my choice. Once I learned to control the wetness, I learned I could control it all."

"Are we still talking about painting here?" Emily said, with a smile. *I can't believe that came out of my mouth. Oh my God. Stop it! Stop it!* She felt her face burn.

"Maybe not. What do you say we finish these and take a walk on the canal?"

Over Emily's weak objection, Sarah pulled two bills out of her purse and laid them on the bar to cover their tab. Emily wasn't at all sure of the proper protocol for such things when on a date with a woman. For that matter, she still wasn't positive this was a date, so she didn't press the issue. On the way out, she dropped the bartender's business card into the trash.

The evening air had a hint of fall but was still warm enough for a pleasant walk without the need for a coat. The moon, a quarter full, shone bright in the sky. It cast a lovely glow over the canal, across the street from Rumors.

Sarah reached out and took Emily's hand, entwining their fingers together.

Okay, I am thinking definite date here. Heat rose in Emily, then cooled, leaving a trail of goose bumps on her arms. *Oh damn, this is a date. Okay, what should I do? I'm thinking throwing up wouldn't be a good idea. Calm down, calm down. It's just a date. A date with a woman! I can do this. I can do this. Can I do this? Yes, I can do this. Oh my God. I'm not sure I can do this.*

Emily wasn't sure if the light-headedness she felt was due to the wine or the fact that the hand that she held belonged to a female. She wasn't a big drinker, and this was the second night in a row that she had shared wine with a beautiful woman. Her thoughts went to Andi and the feelings that had come to life with a simple foot rub, feelings she had pushed down because they frightened her. *I am done being afraid.* Her mind was still with

Andi when Sarah pulled her by the hand off the pathway and behind a tree. She gently pushed Emily against the rough bark and leaned into her. When their lips met, Emily told herself again that she was done being afraid. She closed her eyes and accepted the gentle kiss.

"I have wanted to do that all evening," Sarah said. When Emily didn't voice any objections, Sarah kissed her again with more pressure, her tongue darting out and delicately licking the inside of Emily's lips.

I'm kissing a woman, her tongue tentatively meeting Sarah's. A flood of sensations ran through her body. Her heart pounded as blood coursed into areas that had long lain dormant. Emily ran her fingers through Sarah's hair and pulled her face in closer. Emily's body was taking over, her own thoughts pushed aside.

Her ringing phone jerked her out of the trance and she released Sarah's hair as their lips parted. Emily silently apologized with her eyes as she struggled to catch her breath before answering the phone.

"Hello." Her voice quavered.

"Hi, Emily." It was Mindy. "Are you gonna be back? Daddy gotta movie, and we want you to s-s-see it too."

Emily's mind scrambled for an answer. "Sure, honey. I'll be there in a little while. Go ahead and start the movie, and you and Dad watch it. You can catch me up on what I missed when I get there." She struggled to keep her voice even and her thoughts coherent.

"Come now. I do not want you to miss some."

"I'll be there soon, okay? I'll see you in a little while. Bye." Emily was reluctant to leave, but she knew she had to. This was going much too fast for her, and she needed time to think and figure this out.

"You're going to call it a night, huh?" Emily could hear the disappointment in Sarah's voice.

"I'm so sorry. I had a wonderful time, but yeah, I really should get going."

"Can I talk you into meeting me at my studio in the morning? I'll bring breakfast."

Emily couldn't seem to resist the sparkle in her eyes, visible even in the moonlight. "Don't you have to be at the festival in the morning?"

"Lauren's watching my booth until noon, so no. I don't have to be there in the morning." She raised her eyebrows, waited for an answer.

"In that case, I would love to." She wasn't sure if it was her brain or her body answering. Sarah leaned in and kissed Emily again, softly on the lips. The rush of electricity once more surged through Emily. Never mind, it was definitely her body that had answered.

"Come on, I'll walk you to your car." She took Emily's hand and led her back to the parking lot.

"I'll call you in the morning with directions, if that's all right." Sarah swept a single finger across Emily's cheek, leaving a hot trail in its wake.

Emily nodded, finding it difficult to form words.

"I think we can have some fun," Sarah said. She turned and walked away.

Emily stood for several seconds watching her go. She realized as she slipped into the driver's seat of her car that she was wet. Wet from *kissing* another woman. She'd had the same reaction to Andi rubbing her feet. She had to be well on the way to third base with her ex-husband before her body would even start to react. *I need to see where this leads.* Fear or no fear, it was time to figure this out. Time to try taking another step out of her comfort zone. No. Doing a couple pieces of art in a different medium was stepping out of her comfort zone. This was more like leaping off a cliff. Emily hoped she didn't break her neck on the landing.

❖

The movie was more than half over by the time Emily walked into the house.

Mindy shook her head in an obvious attempt to reprimand her, but couldn't pull it off for long. She lapsed into giggles. "Sit down, Emily. I tell you about the movie. Daddy, pause it, please."

Without objection, Emily did as she was told. It seemed to take Mindy forever to relay the details of the story. She went on and on and Emily had trouble making sense of it. Her thoughts drifted back to Sarah and she stifled a smile.

"...and then the bad guy, that one there," she said pointing to the man frozen on the television screen, "he put them puppies all in a big cage. Okay, ready, 'cause that is where we s-s-stopped. Here we go. Hit it, Daddy."

Emily couldn't focus on the images flickering by on the TV screen. Her mind was somewhere else. The tree. Her back pressed against it. Sarah's lips pressed against hers.

She lay in bed later that night, replaying the kiss in her mind. The reaction of her body was unmistakable. She felt a surge in her belly and below. She tried to make sense of it all. No matter how many different ways she tried to explain it away or make excuses, there was only one conclusion she could come to. She was gay. The simple act of a kiss had been earth-shattering for her. It had all seemed so natural and right. In an instant, it had changed the way she viewed herself and opened up a world of possibilities. The thought made her giddy with excitement. She thought of Sarah and her soft blond hair and her even softer lips and smiled in the dark.

But the feelings were pushed aside by a questioning voice in her head. *Am I some kind of an idiot? I must be. How could I go this long in my life and not know I'm gay? I'm thirty-five frickin' years old, for God's sake. How could I not have known? Maybe I did know it. Maybe I just wouldn't admit it to myself. I never really enjoyed sex with men, but I thought there was something wrong with me. Oh my God, I guess there is something wrong with me. I'm gay. Stop it! Being gay doesn't mean there's something wrong with you. You've known gay people and you never thought there was anything wrong with them. You know Andi and she's gay and there is absolutely nothing wrong with her. She's wonderful. Andi. Andi was kissing someone. Andi. No. Sarah was kissing me. Sarah, who has soft lips, was kissing me. I need to talk to Mom about this.*

But she couldn't.

Her mother was dead.

Emily had had a lot of moments like this. Her world crashed down around her as she realized, once again, the reality of her loss. This time, the reality that her mother was gone seemed to hit her with even greater force. It knocked the wind out of her, taking her breath away. She wouldn't be talking to her mother about this. She wouldn't be talking to her about anything ever again. A tear ran down her cheek, followed by another and another until she was sobbing.

Would her mother have understood and accepted these new revelations about Emily? She had been so nervous when she told her mother that she was divorcing Brian. Emily had been raised in a church that said divorce was wrong. She was afraid that her mother would adopt that idea and tell Emily that she shouldn't do it. Instead, her mother hugged her and told her she loved her. "God doesn't want you to be unhappy, baby, and neither do I. You need to do what's best for you." She had accepted Emily's need to get out of that marriage and she would have accepted this too. Emily was sure of it—almost.

"You're going to look like shit in the morning if you don't stop crying and get some sleep," she said out loud. She pulled a few tissues out of the box on the nightstand and wiped her eyes. She flipped on the lamp and looked around the room. Her childhood bedroom. Her parents hadn't changed it much after she left for college. The pale pink walls had faded over the years. Her books lined up on a small bookcase in the corner were long ago forgotten and more than a little dusty. A single poster was thumbtacked to the wall over the desk. It had hung there since she was sixteen. She laughed out loud at the significance of it. Something that had evaded her until now. While her friends were putting up posters of guys in rock bands and pictures of Tom Cruise, her poster was of Julia Roberts. *I wish I had realized a long time ago that I have a predisposition for pretty women. I guess there were a lot of things I didn't realize.*

She turned the lamp off again, plunging the room into darkness. Staring into the nothingness, she thought about her life and all of the clues she had missed that held the truth of who she was. Tomorrow she would begin living that truth. Tomorrow she would be seeing Sarah again. Tomorrow. She closed her eyes and when she opened them again, it would be tomorrow.

CHAPTER EIGHT

I'll pick you up at one," Emily reminded Mindy. Mindy skipped from the car down the Burtons' driveway and knocked on the front door. Timmy Burton pushed passed his mother as she opened the door. He threw his arms around Mindy and hugged her. Timmy, like Mindy, had Down syndrome. They'd been classmates in school, and Mindy often referred to him as her *best friend*.

Emily returned the wave from Timmy's mother, waited until Mindy was safely inside and pulled back out onto the road. The directions to Sarah's studio were easy enough. It was in a large building off Goodman Street, down the road from the Clothesline Art Festival. Emily took mostly back roads to get there, trying to avoid some of the downtown congestion around the art gallery.

She pulled into the mostly empty parking lot. *Deep breath. It's all good. Nothing to worry about.* Emily took several more deep breaths in an attempt to calm herself. *Okay, let's do this.* She pushed the butterflies down, silently cursing them.

She wasn't sure she could manage walking up four flights of stairs and still be able to breathe when she reached the top, so she opted for the only other choice: an old freight elevator. The large elevator doors were open when she entered the building. She walked in and pulled on the thick canvas strap that hung down from the large metal door. The top half of the door came down to meet the bottom half as it rose up. She pulled on a second strap and a wire door came down with a loud clang, startling her. It took a few seconds for the elevator to start moving after she pushed the button with the four nearly worn away. It moved much smoother than Emily thought it would, given its obvious age.

The look of the hallway on the fourth floor was very different from the dilapidated look of the elevator. Fresh blue paint greeted her, and to her delight, beautifully framed artwork adorned the walls. A small cardboard sign with neatly handwritten letters pointed the way.

Emily turned to the right and continued down the hall. She glanced at the artwork as she passed and read the numbers on the doors. She came upon a watercolor painting and immediately recognized the style. It was Sarah's. The open door to the studio was up ahead on the right, and Emily could hear music coming from the room.

Emily took the last few steps to the open door and paused. *Damn. I didn't even think to bring anything. Should I have brought flowers or cinnamon toast or something? Maybe I can offer her a kidney.* She giggled to herself as her nerves bubbled to the surface again. With slight hesitation, Emily knocked.

Sarah set a large frame down against the wall and turned. Her face lit up with a smile and she walked to Emily with open arms. She pulled her into a quick hug. "Welcome. Come in, come in." Sarah closed the door behind her.

"This is great." Emily took in the large room. Several tall windows starting a few feet from the floor reached up to the ceiling on one wall. Tables and easels were set up in various positions to take advantage of the sunlight coming in. Only a few paintings hung on the walls, but there were empty hooks where other paintings had been. *Probably in Sarah's booth at the Clothesline show*, Emily reasoned. A love seat and couch sat facing each other off to one side, a coffee table in between them.

Emily gave Sarah a tentative smile. She was trying to decide if she should mention that she had never dated a woman before. Before she could decide, Sarah took her hand and led her to the couch.

"Come, sit, I got us some bagels and strawberry cream cheese. I hope that's okay."

Emily sat and Sarah crossed the studio to get the food. Emily found her eyes roaming over Sarah's backside. *Oh my God. Just because you think you're a lesbian now doesn't mean you can stare at a woman's butt*, Emily reprimanded herself. But she didn't take her eyes away until Sarah turned around, a Wegmans bakery bag in hand. Two bagels, cream cheese, and a plastic knife appeared from the bag, and Sarah set them on the table.

"I have a fresh pot of coffee or orange juice. Which would you prefer?"

Emily cleared her throat in an attempt to clear away the jitters. "Juice would be great."

Sarah poured a cup of coffee for herself and juice for Emily. She set the drinks down on the table and sat next to Emily.

"So, how are you?" Sarah rested her hand on Emily's knee.

Emily couldn't help but smile. "Good. I had a nice time last night."

"Me too." Sarah went to work spreading cream cheese on the bagels and handed one to Emily.

Emily took a bite. She hadn't had a fresh Wegmans bagel since she had moved to Syracuse. Not that they didn't have Wegmans here, it was just closer to go to Tops to shop.

"Mmm. That is so good. Thank you." She licked her lips to get a bit of cream cheese that escaped her mouth.

"My pleasure." Sarah reached over and wiped a small drop of cream cheese from Emily's lip with her finger. "You missed some." She brought the finger to her own mouth.

Emily licked her lips again as she watched Sarah's mouth. "Um, thanks. Would you like a kidney?" Her mouth went suddenly dry.

"What?" Sarah said, with a little laugh.

"Oh my God. I can't believe I said that. It was just a little joke, but it sounded so much funnier in my head."

"I'm very interested in your body." Sarah raised her eyebrows. "But it isn't your kidneys I'm after."

Emily felt a blush rise to her cheeks, not sure how to respond. Her body, however, knew exactly how to respond. A jolt of electricity traveled through her and settled squarely in her crotch. But for some reason, that didn't help her find any words to say.

"I'm sorry," Sarah said. "Clearly, I've made you uncomfortable. I didn't mean to do that."

"No, it's okay." Emily felt foolish.

"Are you going back to Syracuse tonight?" Sarah said, changing the direction of the conversation.

"Yes." Emily was grateful for the change. "I have to be back at work in the morning. We'll be leaving after dinner with my father."

"Would it be okay if I called you sometime?"

"I would be disappointed if you didn't."

"What would you think if I came to visit? I was thinking maybe on Friday. I have an art show at the Rochester Public Market next Sunday, but have Friday and most of Saturday free."

"I think I would like that very much," Emily said. She definitely wanted to get to know this woman better. She felt like the conversations up to this point had been pretty much superficial. They had talked mostly about art. She would like to know more about the person, not just the artist.

"So, tell me about your job. What kind of classes are you teaching? Painting? Drawing?" The conversation turned back to art. At least the topic was comfortable.

"I teach oil painting, watercolor, color theory…"

Sarah leaned over without warning and kissed her. She wrapped her arms around Emily and pulled her in close.

Emily barely had enough presence of mind to set her bagel down before running her hands over Sarah's back. Again, Emily's body responded in a way that still surprised and shocked her. When Sarah's tongue entered her mouth, Emily thought she was going to explode. She wanted more. She wanted Sarah's hands on her. She wanted to feel what it felt like to be with a woman. But she knew she couldn't let that happen. Not now. Not so soon after meeting someone. As turned on as she felt, she didn't want to make love with someone she barely knew. She fought to tame her body's sensations, but she felt a surge of moisture. *Oh shit. This isn't working very well.*

Her hands had a mind of their own and she was astonished when they made their way around Sarah's waist and up her sides. Sarah's hands covered Emily's and nudged them upward until they were on her breasts. She could feel Sarah's nipples harden as her hands ran over the thin material of the blouse and bra that separated her hands from skin. Another rush of her own wetness told her just how turned on she was from touching this woman. She wanted to feel skin. She was sure she wouldn't be able to control her hands any longer, and she was right. They traveled back down to Sarah's waist and came up again, this time under Sarah's shirt. She let out a low moan, directly into Sarah's mouth, when her hands touched skin, soft skin, smooth skin, Sarah's skin.

It's only her waist. I'm touching her waist and my fingers feel like they're on fire. What have I been missing all these years? She willed herself to stop, but it didn't look like that was going to happen anytime soon. Her hands traveled up that warm, hot back and reached behind Sarah for her bra clasp. She unhooked it in one quick move. Her fingertips swept around to the front, reached up under the now loose bra, and cupped Sarah's firm breasts in her hands.

It was Sarah's turn to moan and she tipped her head back as the sound escaped her throat. Emily took the opportunity to kiss Sarah's long neck. She kissed and licked down to the hollow at the base of her neck and lingered there. Sarah brought Emily's face back up and kissed her again. Their tongues tumbled together inside Emily's mouth and Emily began to feel light-headed. Her hands danced over Sarah's breasts. Her palms rubbed against the tight nipples as her fingers squeezed the soft flesh surrounding them.

Sarah removed her own shirt and discarded it on the floor. Her bra quickly followed. She tugged Emily's T-shirt from her waistband and pulled it up, leaving it gathered at Emily's neck. Sarah wasted no time unhooking Emily's bra and pushing it up as well. Sarah pushed Emily back on the couch and in one quick motion was on top of her, never breaking the contact of their lips. Emily could feel Sarah's firm, round breasts covering hers. She delighted in the feeling. *No wonder Andi likes…* Her thoughts flashed to Andi and someone kissing Andi in the front seat of that car yesterday morning. Her breath caught in her throat. She needed to stop. She needed to breathe.

"We need to slow down," she managed to say.

"Okay. Whatever you want," Sarah said, with obvious difficulty. She slowed the roaming of her hands on Emily's breasts and brought her mouth back to Emily's and kissed her again, this time with less urgency and more tenderness.

Emily pulled her head back. "No, I mean we have to stop. We need to slow down on everything. This is going way too fast for me. I'm sorry." Emily knew she was just as responsible for letting it get this far as Sarah was, maybe more so. The last thing she wanted to be was a tease. "I'm sorry," Emily repeated.

Sarah sat up. "No, no, don't apologize. I'm the one who's sorry. You are just so beautiful that I got carried away. We can go as slow as you want." Sarah picked up her shirt and bra and put them back on.

Emily remained lying back on the couch for several seconds, trying to get her thoughts together before sitting up. It took her another few moments to realize that her shirt was still up around her neck and her bra was hanging loose. In quick succession, she hooked her bra and pulled down her shirt. She could feel the heat seeping up from her chest into her face. She avoided eye contact with Sarah in a vain attempt to hide her embarrassment.

"It's all right. Really." Sarah smiled and gave Emily's hand a squeeze. "Really," she repeated. "Let's finish breakfast." She handed Emily her bagel, picked up her own, and took a bite. Her eyes never left Emily.

Emily took a sip of her orange juice, waiting for her heart to stop racing. She forced herself to make eye contact and nibbled on her bagel. They finished eating, making light conversation. The topic didn't stray far from superficial.

"I'll call you in a few days if that's still all right," Sarah said. She walked Emily to the door.

"Yes, please call." Emily smiled. She gave Sarah a kiss on the cheek and left. Walking past the elevator, she chose the stairs in an attempt to work off some of the massive amount of energy coursing through her.

Back in her car, she leaned her head against the headrest and closed her eyes. *Wow.* She couldn't believe that had happened. Couldn't believe how it made her feel. *Wow, wow, wow.* She drove around aimlessly for about an hour before heading the car in the direction of her father's house.

❖

"So, how are you doing, Dad?" Emily passed him the salad, glad to be having dinner as a family.

"Not great. But, doing a little better every day. I have thirty-five days under my belt with AA." He gave her a tired smile.

"That's great, Dad," Emily said.

"What is AA?" Mindy asked. "Is it like when your c-c-car breaks down?"

Emily couldn't help but smile. "No, sweetie, that's triple A. Remember we talked about Daddy having some problems with being so sad?" She looked at her father, and he nodded for her to continue. "He was drinking a little too much beer and stuff like that and it wasn't good for him. AA is like a club that helps him get better."

"You feel better, Daddy?" Mindy asked, between bites of food.

"I sure do, kiddo. But I miss you guys."

"We will visit you lots so you don't have to m-m-miss us too much. Okay, Daddy?" She got up and hugged him. "Don't be sad."

"Thanks, baby. Now go eat the rest of your dinner."

Mindy released his neck and trotted back to her seat.

"I'm sorry, Dad. You know I never would have taken a job so far away if I had known what was going to happen to Mom. I needed a change after everything with Brian." Guilt swept through her like a windstorm.

"I know. It was a good change for you. I'm glad you did it. But that doesn't mean I can't miss ya." He winked at her. His eyes looked clearer than they had a couple of months ago. He'd even shaved before he and Mindy went to church that morning. "You also might be interested to know that I've taken care of all the paperwork from the funeral home, insurance policies and everything else. Well, most of it. There is just so much of it to do. I'll tell ya, it has been quite a chore. But I am proud to say it's almost done." His smile looked genuine. "Your mother would have died if she knew it cost a hundred and fifty dollars to do her hair for the funeral." It was a good sign that he was making light of it.

"Holy c-c-cow," Mindy said. "A hundred and fifty d-d-dollars? When I have a funeral, somebody better bring a brush to brush my hair." Everyone laughed.

"That won't be for a long, long time, kiddo."

"Okay, Daddy. Do I have to eat these b-b-beans? They are all mushy." Mindy made a face.

"They're supposed to be mushy. They're baked beans. But no, you don't have to eat them if you don't like 'em. It won't hurt my feelings none, even though I did spend all of three minutes opening the can and heating them up. But that's okay, don't eat 'em if ya don't like 'em," he teased.

"Oh, Daddy, you are funny."

Emily tuned out of the conversation as her mind skipped ahead. Tomorrow was Monday and she couldn't wait to talk to Andi and tell her about Sarah.

CHAPTER NINE

It was tough getting through the first three periods at school Monday morning. Nerves, anxiety, and excitement took turns coursing through Emily's body and mind. The message she'd left on Andi's voice mail said to meet her in the art room at lunchtime. She wanted so badly to talk to her. Emily decided not to ask Andi about the kiss she'd witnessed in the parking lot on Saturday morning. In fact, she decided not to think about it at all. It was time to concentrate on her own life. Emily hadn't told anyone about her self-revelation, and she wanted—no, she needed—to talk to someone. And her first choice, maybe her only choice, was Andi.

Andi knocked once and let herself into the art room. "What's up?" she asked. "You sounded a little weird on the phone. Is everything all right?" She shut the door behind her.

Emily didn't say anything. She wasn't sure how to start.

Andi plopped down on a table across from Emily and waited. No coherent sentences formed in Emily's mind.

"So? Are you going to talk to me? I'm starting to get a little worried here. Em?"

Emily moved to the front of the desk and faced Andi. She looked down and focused on the floor for several long moments as she gathered her thoughts. She lifted her head and looked into Andi's deep brown eyes for a moment. Then she looked at the floor again. This wasn't going to be as easy as she thought. She had never said the words *I'm gay* to anyone before. Hell, she hadn't even considered it as a possibility a week ago.

Emily spoke in hushed tones even though the door was closed. "I think I'm gay," she said meeting Andi's eyes.

Andi paused before speaking. "Are you serious?"

"Yes."

Andi visibly swallowed. She took Emily's hand. "Em, I—"

"I met someone," Emily interrupted her. She waited for Andi's response. When she didn't get one, she went on. "Well, what do you think? Tell me what you're thinking."

A look of disappointment crossed Andi's face, but it disappeared as quickly as it came. She smiled, but the smile never quite reached her eyes. "Who is she? Where did you meet her?"

Emily thought about it for a second. She realized that she didn't have a whole lot to tell because she didn't know that much about Sarah. "She's an artist and I met her at an art festival in Rochester this past weekend. She's blond and pretty, and her sister lives across the street from my dad."

"That's great." Andi's eyes lacked their usual sparkle. Emily didn't know what to make of it. "An artist, huh? So you have something in common."

"Yeah."

"Can I ask you a personal question?"

"No, I didn't sleep with her, but we did kiss and it was, well…it was surprising and it was wonderful."

Andi struggled to keep any hint of emotion from her voice. She was confused and more than a little disappointed. "Thanks for sharing, but that wasn't going to be my question. I was going to ask you how come all of a sudden you are interested in women. In this woman?" This woman? *What is it about* this *woman?*

"I'm not sure. I guess I've had feelings for women all my life but never let myself realize what it all meant. I don't think I ever allowed it to be a possibility in my mind before. I met Sarah at the festival and she asked me out. Well, I wasn't sure if she was asking me out or to have a drink with her as a friend. Anyway, I went, and she kissed me. Andi, I have never had my body react like that before. I have never—I mean, it was just a kiss, and my body, I mean my whole body…" A deep blush crept up Emily's neck to her face.

"I know what you mean," Andi said. "I know how it feels when that happens, especially if the only experience you've had up to this point is with the wrong gender." Could it be true? Could Emily really be gay or was she just—

"Yes, I knew if anyone would understand, it would be you."

"So, you really like this woman?" Andi asked, hoping the answer would be no. But she could tell by the look on Emily's face that she did.

"Yes. I mean, I like what I know so far. She seems nice. I don't really know a lot about her, but I want to get to know her better."

"I am very happy for you, Emily. You deserve the best." Andi meant it. Most of it.

Emily hugged her tightly. "Thank you. She may come to visit this weekend."

"This weekend, huh?"

"Yes. Do you want to meet her?"

Not really. "Sure, at some point. But why don't you take this weekend for yourselves? I can take Mindy if you want me to. I have to help my friend, Taylor, with a few things right after work on Friday, but I can pick Mindy up after that." Andi's voice cracked the slightest bit. She cleared her throat.

"Wow. That would be great. You wouldn't mind? Are you sure?" Emily sounded downright giddy.

Yeah. No. Actually I don't want to take Mindy. I don't want you to see this woman. I want you to see me.

"Are you sure?" Emily repeated.

Andi silently reprimanded herself. *Emily is your friend. You want her to be happy. Apparently this woman makes her happy.* Andi straightened her back and sucked in her feelings. "No problem at all. I love that kid, you know. We can go to the movies and eat popcorn till we're sick."

Emily gave her a look that spoke volumes.

"Okay, maybe that last part isn't a good idea. How about I take her to a movie and buy her a *little* popcorn?"

"You're the best." Emily hugged her again. Andi found herself leaning into it, feeling the heat from Emily's body mixing with her own. She knew a few more seconds in this position, and she would have a problem letting go. She pulled back and looked into Emily's eyes, saw the excitement radiating out. She cared about Emily enough to want her to be happy. Andi decided to do whatever she could to make sure that happened.

CHAPTER TEN

You've got to be kidding me," Taylor said, as she handed a box labeled *DISHES* to Andi. Andi set it on the counter and opened the top.

"Nope. She said she's gay, and she found someone she likes." Andi shook her head.

"Oh man, I'm so sorry. I could tell from the way you talked about her that you like her."

"I did my best not to, but yeah, I did. I do. I mean, what the hell?" She took a stack of dessert plates out of the box and carefully removed the packing paper around them. "I had no idea she was gay, so there was no way I was going to tell her that."

"Why don't you tell her now?" Taylor grabbed another box from the stack on the floor and put it on the table. She leaned on it as she waited for Andi's answer.

"No way. I don't think that's the right thing to do. She seems to really like this woman. Sarah."

Taylor opened her mouth and put her finger in it, pretending to vomit. "Sarah smara. The hell with Sarah. Tell her."

This conversation wasn't what she needed right now. Andi just needed someone to listen. She had already decided she wasn't going to tell Emily about her feelings. Emily had enough confusing stuff going on. Andi wasn't going to add to that. "How come I'm the only one unpacking boxes?" Andi asked in an effort to change the subject.

"Because this is more important." Taylor wasn't about to let this go. "You didn't have any idea that she played on our team?"

"She didn't even have an idea. How was I supposed to?" Andi continued unpacking the box in front of her. She nodded to the box in front of Taylor in a weak attempt to get her do the same.

This was the third time in two years that Taylor had moved into a new apartment, and her other friends were apparently tired of helping her unpack. Andi had to leave soon to pick up Mindy, and she wanted to get as much done here as possible.

Besides, she had already spent the last four days turning this over in her mind. She couldn't tell Emily about her feelings when she thought Emily was straight and she couldn't tell her now because she was dating someone. Life was so unfair sometimes.

"So what are you going to do?" Taylor asked.

"I'm going to unpack this box." She knew damn well that wasn't what Taylor meant.

"About Emily." She let out an exasperated breath.

"I'm going to be her friend. I'm going to support her in whatever she decides." *And I'm going to hope my heart can take it.*

❖

Emily was both excited and nervous to see Sarah again. It was all arranged. Andi said she would pick Mindy up at six, and Sarah was expected around seven. Emily wanted to take this weekend to really get to know Sarah better. She decided that she would sleep in Mindy's room and give Sarah her room. She didn't want anything to get out of hand. She'd waited this long to figure out she was gay. She could wait a little longer to make love with a woman. She wanted to be in love, or at least in strong *like*, before she did.

Mindy was already home and packing an overnight bag

when Emily got home from work. Emily could hear her singing in her room.

"Do you have your toothbrush packed?" Emily asked, leaning against the doorjamb of Mindy's room.

"Yes." Her annoyance was evident in the look she gave Emily.

Emily ignored the look. "How about clean underwear?"

"Umm, I was getting that." Mindy opened her dresser drawer and pawed through her underwear until she came upon her purple pair. She unzipped the canvas duffel bag, stuffed the underwear in, and zipped the bag closed again.

"How about clean socks?"

Mindy walked back to her dresser and pulled out a pair of pink socks and added them to the duffel bag.

"How about pajamas?" Mindy gave her that look again.

"Of course I have my p-p-pajamas. I not a little kid, you know." She picked up the duffel bag and grabbed her Dora the Explorer pillow from the bed. Mindy pushed past Emily to wait for Andi in the living room.

Emily followed and handed her two twenty-dollar bills. "Use this to pay for the movie and popcorn. Tell Andi it's your treat."

Mindy looked confused. "My tweet?"

Emily couldn't help but laugh. "You say, *it's my treat.* Never mind. Just tell Andi that you are paying for the movie and popcorn. Okay?"

"Okay. Can I keep the change?"

"You can keep the change, but don't use it to buy candy or anything else at the theater. You can get a small popcorn and a soda and let Andi get anything she wants."

"How come she gets anything s-s-she wants and I only can get small popcorn and soda?"

"Mindy." Emily tried to say it with authority, but it came out a little weak. "Please do what I ask you, okay? Promise?"

"Okay, okay, okay, I p-promise. Get off my case." Mindy

giggled, unable to pull off the authoritative voice she obviously
strived for.

The doorbell rang. "Andi!" Mindy yelled and ran to let her
in. She shook Andi's hand politely before giving her a big hug.

"How ya doing, sweetie? Ready for a girls' night out?"

"Yeah. We gonna do a girls' night out." Mindy seemed over
the moon to be spending time with her newest *best friend*. "I have
to get my s-s-suitcase." Mindy ran back into the living room,
followed closely by Andi.

"Hey, hot stuff, are you ready for your evening?" Andi said,
when she saw Emily.

"Ready as I'll ever be." She smiled and leaned in to give
Andi a hug.

"Need any advice?" Andi whispered, close to her ear. Her
breath was warm on Emily's skin and the warmth traveled down
Emily's body.

"Nothing is going to happen," Emily whispered back.
She looked directly into Andi's brown eyes. "Nothing is going
to happen," she repeated. She wasn't sure if she was trying to
convince Andi or herself.

"Okay," Andi said to Emily. She turned to Mindy. "Are you
ready?"

Mindy held tight to her duffel bag and pillow. "Yep."

"Okay, tell your sister goodbye, and let's get going." Mindy
gave Emily a hug and linked her arm in Andi's. At the door, Andi
handed her the keys. "Press this button right here." Andi pointed.
"And it'll unlock the doors. Put your stuff in the back seat and I'll
be out in a second."

Once Mindy left Andi turned her attention back to Emily.
"Are you all set? Are you all right?" She rubbed Emily's arm and
left a trail of goose bumps.

"I am *so* nervous, but I'm okay. Everything will be fine.
Thank you so much. I mean that. Thank you." She gave Andi a
kiss on the cheek.

"Call me if you need anything."

"Like what?"

"I don't know…anything."

"Thank you."

"You got it. Have a wonderful evening. I'll see you sometime late tomorrow afternoon."

Emily closed the door behind her and leaned her head against it. *I hope I'm doing the right thing here.* She wondered why, all of a sudden, these doubts were springing up. Well, doubts or not, she had company coming in an hour and she wanted to be ready. She thought about what still needed to be done. The house was clean, the wine was chilling and dinner was put together. She would put it in the oven after Sarah arrived. She was ready. *What am I ready for? Am I jumping into this too fast? Am I ready for this relationship? Is it a relationship?* No, it was too early for that. But it could be, someday. She was ready to find out where this led. Maybe.

Emily decided to change out of her work clothes into something a little more casual. She chose a pair of black jeans and coral cotton shirt. Barefooted, she trotted to the bathroom, washed her face, brushed her hair and teeth. She applied a thin layer of foundation, mascara, and blush, checked herself one more time in the mirror, and nodded her approval.

❖

Emily checked the wall clock for the fifteenth time. She brushed her teeth again, straightened the couch cushions, adjusted a picture on the wall. She was running out of things to fuss with. At seven fifteen she heard a knock on the door and jumped.

Calm down, calm down, calm down. Okay, I'm calm. Who am I kidding? Just be yourself. But not your normal scaredy-cat, chickenshit self. Okay, stop it.

Emily opened the door. "Hello," she said to Sarah. "Welcome to my humble abode."

"Hi," Sarah said. She looked Emily up and down. "You look great."

Emily liked the attention and at the same time felt a little exposed the way Sarah looked at her. It made her nervous.

"So do you," Emily said, looking directly at her eyes, avoiding the full body scan Sarah had done. "Come on in."

Sarah looked around as she entered. "Very nice place." She looked casually elegant in a cream-colored satin blouse neatly tucked into navy blue dress pants.

"Thanks. I like it. Sit down and I'll go get us some wine and put supper in the oven. We can eat in about an hour." Emily went into the kitchen, glad to have a few minutes to compose herself. *Stopped being so anxious*, she told herself. *You are going to look like a dork if you don't get a grip.*

Emily found the corkscrew in the drawer and, after several failed attempts, got the cork out of the wine bottle, breaking it into several pieces. She poured the wine into two glasses and used her fingers to remove the small pieces of cork that floated on top. *Andi wouldn't have broken the cork into pieces.*

Andi…

Stop thinking about Andi!

She swallowed hard and turned her thoughts back to Sarah as she continued gathering the appetizers she'd made earlier and putting dinner in the oven.

Holding a plate of hors d'oeuvres in one hand, she carefully picked up the two glasses of wine, holding the stems between her fingers. She walked back to the living room, trying not to spill anything, and amazingly, succeeded.

"Let me help you." Sarah got up and took both glasses. Emily noticed she had slipped off her high-heeled shoes and set them off to the side of the couch.

Emily put the plate down on the coffee table and accepted her glass of wine back from Sarah.

"Cheers," Sarah said, clinking her glass gently against Emily's.

Emily sipped her wine, hoping it would lessen the feeling like she was crawling out of her skin. *It's because I haven't eaten since lunch*, Emily told herself. Maybe that was why she felt a little sick. No. It wasn't an empty stomach. When would she accept that anything new made her nervous? And this was definitely something new.

Emily offered Sarah an appetizer. Sarah took one and nibbled on it. Emily took two and ate the first one in two bites, before starting on the next. That didn't help her stomach any. Maybe more wine would help.

"I like your use of light in your painting." Sarah pointed to a landscape on the wall. "I assume you painted it."

Emily nodded and continued to sip her wine, watching Sarah over the rim of her glass. *She certainly is pretty.*

"I can feel the exact time of day that was."

"Thank you," Emily said. She set her glass of wine down, realizing she had already consumed half of it. If she didn't slow down she would be drunk before they even got to dinner. Silence filled the air for several seconds. Several *long* seconds. "So, you have an art show on Sunday?" Emily said, feeling the need to fill the gap with conversation.

"Yes. I'm really hoping for nice weather. Last year was so cold."

Emily was hoping for deeper conversation but couldn't quite get more personal questions out of her mouth. Sarah seemed content with surface talk.

"Would you like more wine?" Emily asked, picking up her own glass again.

"Not right now. I still have plenty left. I'll have another glass with dinner."

"It should be ready soon. So, Sarah…" *Why is this so hard?*
"Yes?"

"Have you lived in Rochester all your life?" *Lame.*
"Born and raised."

Several long seconds went by. Emily sipped her wine.

"Emily, I know you said you want to go slow, but I was wondering if it would be all right if I kissed you?"

"Yes," Emily answered. There would be no need for talking if her mouth was covered by Sarah's. A tingle ran through her at the mere thought of it.

Without another word, Sarah kissed her. Emily closed her eyes as their lips met. It was soft and slow and easy. Easy. It was so easy to kiss Sarah, too easy. Much easier than talking. The kiss deepened. Sarah pulled Emily in closer, and Emily could feel Sarah's soft breasts pushing against hers. When Sarah's tongue entered her mouth, she melted.

Emily wasn't sure who started it this time, but before she knew what was happening, both women had shed their shirts. Emily found herself on her back with Sarah on top of her. Sarah's mouth moved down from Emily's lips to her neck. They traveled farther down to Emily's breasts, and Emily let out a deep moan as warm lips circled her nipple.

This is what it should feel like. Hot. Electric. A woman had her mouth on her. *A woman. This is the way it's supposed to be.*

Sarah's mouth paused briefly as she said, "We can do whatever you're comfortable with. I won't push you. I just enjoy being with a woman so much more than sex with my husband."

What? That's not the way it's supposed to be. Emily wasn't sure she had heard Sarah correctly. "What? Your husband?"

Sarah's tongue traveled up Emily's neck and stopped at her chin. "Yeah. I prefer sleeping with women. Don't get me wrong, I love my husband and sex with him is great, but it's so much better with a woman. You know? Soft and everything."

In one quick move, Emily extracted herself from Sarah and stood up. "You're married?"

"Yes. I thought you knew that." Sarah sat up.

"And how would I have known that?" Emily did her best to keep the tears she felt welling up in her eyes from spilling out. *What the hell am I doing? What the hell kind of game is this?*

"You know my sister, so I assumed you knew I was married.

My husband is the one who recommended that you and I go to Rumors last week."

"You're married and your husband *knows* you do this? He knows about me?" Emily was bewildered and hurt. And a little disgusted at the thought of Sarah's husband knowing what they were doing, what Emily had allowed—*allowed*—with someone who was practically a stranger.

Sarah reached for Emily's hand. "I'm sorry. I wasn't trying to deceive you. I like you and thought we could have some fun together."

Emily pulled her hand away and waved it through the air. "So, this is just for fun?"

"I thought you knew that."

"I would never have—I'm not that kind of gir...No, I didn't know this was just for fun."

"Emily." Sarah looked stunned. "I really thought you knew."

Emily grabbed her shirt off of the floor and pulled it roughly over her head. "I'm thinking that you should probably go." Emily couldn't stop the tears any longer.

"Emily," Sarah repeated.

"Please." Emily needed to be alone. She needed this woman to leave.

"Are you sure that's what you want?"

"Please leave." Emily didn't try to hide the pain in her voice.

Sarah gathered her clothes from the floor and slipped them back on. "I never meant to hurt you."

When Emily didn't respond, Sarah picked up her shoes and walked to the door. She turned as if she was going to say something, changed her mind and left, her shoes still in her hand.

Emily slumped down on the couch. "I am so stupid." She hit the palm of her hand against her forehead with each word. "Stupid, stupid, stupid."

The tears began to flow in earnest. Emily brushed them away with a sudden realization: she was hurt, but in truth, she barely knew the woman who had just walked out that door. Apparently, she knew even less about her than she'd thought. She was crying over the loss of a fantasy, not the loss of Sarah. *That still makes me pretty stupid. Maybe even more so. Okay, so I lost someone I didn't really have and didn't really know. Now what? Well, I won't be jumping into anything else so fast, like an idiot. That's for damn sure.*

Emily had let her body get in the way of her head and her heart. She let long overdue physical feelings dictate her actions. She tried to skip steps and jump ahead to make up for lost time. She had allowed Sarah to touch her, to kiss her. No. *Allowed* wasn't the right word. That made it sound like Sarah had manipulated her. Emily had been a very willing participant in everything that had transpired. She was as much to blame as Sarah. Maybe more so. She wiped away the final tears from her face and blew her nose. She was angrier at herself than at Sarah.

What now? she asked herself. She wasn't going to fall for the next pretty face that came along. Maybe she wouldn't even look at another pretty face. But Emily knew that wasn't true. She knew that she wanted to fall for a pretty face. She wasn't going to settle for the next one or maybe the one after that. She was going to look around and find the *right* pretty face. She would find the woman who was meant for her. Her first question was going to be about marital status. In fact, she was going to start every conversation that way.

Emily was startled out of her thoughts when the timer on the stove blared. "I guess that means dinner's ready," she said sarcastically.

She grabbed her wineglass, went into the kitchen, turned off the timer and oven, and poured herself another glass of wine. Taking the stuffed shells out of the oven, she had the urge to dump the whole thing, pan and all, into the trash. *Very poetic, but not very practical. That would be a waste of perfectly good food.* Instead, she set the pan down on the top of the stove to cool. Emily grabbed her glass of wine and the rest of the bottle and went back into the living room to finish it off. Her thoughts went to Andi and how she would explain what happened tonight. She hoped Andi would understand and not think she was a fool. Andi. Andi was a good friend. Andi *would* understand. Tomorrow. She would tell Andi tomorrow.

She grabbed her laptop and googled *lesbian dating*. There was a whole world out there to explore and she was determined to do just that.

CHAPTER ELEVEN

So? Spill it. How did it go? How come you're here early?"
Andi ushered Emily in and led the way to the kitchen. She
wanted to know out of a sense of morbid curiosity and a desire to
be a good friend, but she didn't really want details. "Want a cup
of coffee?"

"Coffee would be good."

Andi scooped coffee into the filter and filled the pot with
water. "Okay, tell me."

"It didn't go too well." Emily managed a half smile. "Turns
out she's married."

Andi stopped pouring the water into the coffeemaker.
"Married? As in, *married* married? As in, she has a husband
or wife somewhere married? Or married, as in, she is getting a
divorce married?" Andi asked, truly surprised.

"Married, as in, she has a husband somewhere *married*. I'm
assuming in Rochester."

"Holy shit. I'm so sorry. How did you find out?" Andi
resisted the urge to wrap her arms around Emily to comfort
her. The mix of emotions coursing through her were confusing.
Relief. Surprise. Sadness for Emily. Anger at Sarah.

"She said it. She just said it, like it was nothing. There we
are with our shirts off, kissing and…" Emily stopped when she
seemed to realize what she'd said. Her face turned crimson. She

hesitated. "Anyway, she mentioned her husband, like it was no big deal."

"I'm so sorry, Em," Andi said. "At the risk of repeating myself, holy shit. How are you doing? Are you okay? So, you had your shirt off, huh?" That last part stung a little.

"I can't believe I said that." Emily grimaced. "I'm okay. I did a lot of thinking last night. I could kick myself for getting so carried away with Sarah so fast. You know this gay thing is so new to me. I think I jumped in too quick. I was so anxious to get my lesbian life started that I did it all wrong. I know now that what I need to do is play the field, date a bunch of different women. See what's out there in the world. So I signed up for speed dating online last night."

"You what?" Andi stared at her.

"I signed up for speed dating. Lesbian speed dating. I didn't even know there was such a thing. Did you?" Emily didn't wait for an answer. "It's in a little less than two weeks. I found the information online last night. I found a bunch of dating sites and personal ads, although most of them were pretty raunchy. I can't believe how many women post pictures of their vajayjays."

"Vajayjays?"

"Yeah. You know. Their lady bits. A hoo-hoo. One woman called hers a honeypot."

"One woman where?"

"On Craigslist. I would expect that stuff from guys. But from the women?"

"Emily, I don't think that's the best place to be getting educated on this."

Emily ignored her. "Well, anyway, it was still very interesting. I never knew about any of this. There's a whole lesbian world out there, and I want to explore it. You should try the speed dating too." Her excitement about the endless possibilities seemed to have overtaken her disappointment over Sarah. "So, what do you think? Want to try speed dating?"

"No, that's all right, I'll pass." The last thing Andi wanted to do was sit across from strange women making small talk. She wasn't so sure she wanted Emily doing it either, but Emily seemed determined.

"Why? Come on. Do it with me." Emily obviously didn't realize how that sounded until Andi burst out laughing.

"Come here, baby, I'll do it with you," Andi teased, but deep down knew she actually meant it.

Emily could feel the heat rising up from her neck to her face. She put her hands over her face and shook her head. "That didn't come out quite right." She tried to suppress the laughter, but it bubbled up anyway. "So, enough about me. Tell me about the woman you were kissing in the car last weekend?" There it was: the question that had been nagging at her for a week. She tried to convince herself that she really didn't care, but here she was asking the question anyway. Emily was as surprised by the question as Andi appeared to be.

"How did you know about that?"

"Mindy and I stopped for snacks, and I saw you." Her voice betrayed the hurt she still felt, warranted or not. She felt sick to her stomach waiting for the answer, an answer she wasn't sure she wanted to hear. "I'm sorry. Don't answer. It's none of my business who you're seeing."

"Emily, I'm not seeing anyone. I would tell you if I was. What you saw was my ex-girlfriend Janice kissing *me*. Without warning, I might add. A kiss I didn't return and that I didn't want. If you had stuck around for another thirty seconds you would've seen me push her away." Andi sounded angry, which only added to Emily's confusion.

"I'm sorry. I shouldn't have asked."

"I was going to tell you, but you were so excited about everything that was happening in your life, I figured it could wait."

"So you're not getting back together with her?" Emily averted her eyes. Another question she shouldn't be asking. Much to her horror, tears spilled from her eyes.

"No, I'm not." Andi softened. "Why are you getting upset about this? I would have told you if I was seeing someone." She pulled Emily into a hug.

"I don't know what the hell is wrong with me. I think I'm just overtired." The tears continued to fall as Andi held her. It felt good to be so close to her. "I am getting your shoulder all wet."

"That's fine, as long as it's only tears," she teased gently. "Don't wipe your nose on me. I have this thing against snot."

"Then you better hand me a napkin." Emily pulled back. "Because my nose is starting to run."

Andi ripped a piece of paper towel off the roll and handed it to her. Emily wiped her eyes with it before loudly blowing her nose.

"Hey." She rubbed Emily's shoulder. "I'm getting a little worried about you."

Emily wanted to hide from embarrassment. "I'm just tired. Sorry for being such an idiot."

"You may be stupid, but you ain't no idiot," Andi said, in a less-than-perfect Southern accent.

"Jerk." Emily leaned her head on Andi's shoulder. "Thank you for being here for me."

"I'll always be here for you."

"Thank you for being my friend."

"Friend," Andi said, under her breath.

Emily barely heard her. "Take me out."

"What?"

"Take me out," Emily repeated. "To a lesbian bar or a gay bar or whatever it's called."

"You mean on a da—"

"I want to meet women." Emily interrupted. "Gay women. Lesbian women, and I am thinking there may be one or two at a lesbian bar. Come on, let's do it. Let's go."

"I don't think any of them are open right now."

Emily couldn't quite read her expression. "I know they aren't open now, I meant later. Are they open tonight? I mean,

I'm assuming they're open Saturday nights like regular bars, right? See, I don't know anything about this stuff. But I want to find out."

"Yes, they're open."

"Okay, it's settled then. We're going."

"What about Mindy?"

"I am not taking my little sister to a lesbian bar." Emily swatted Andi.

"No, I mean if you and I are out at a bar tonight, where is Mindy going to be?"

"Mindy can stay by herself. She doesn't need someone with her constantly. I wouldn't want to leave her overnight, but she'll be fine for a few hours."

"Okay. She can stay here tonight. Maybe I'll stay with her."

"Oh no, you won't. You're coming with me, and I'll bring Mindy home. That way I can pick out something nice to wear and she'll be home tonight and can go to bed when she wants to. What should I wear? What do the other women usually wear?"

"Flannel."

"Huh?" Emily asked. "Like pajamas?"

"No, more like hunting shirts. Every woman that goes to a lesbian bar has to wear a plaid flannel hunting shirt." Andi didn't crack a smile.

Emily swatted at her again. "You are such a liar."

"I was joking. I'm such a joker." Andi smiled.

"Okay, I'm going to go wake Mindy up and we're going to get out of your hair."

"Would you like breakfast before you go?"

Emily thought about it. "No, you've done enough for us. I appreciate the offer, but we'll get something to eat at home." She hugged Andi. "Thanks for everything you've done for me."

Andi didn't say anything. She just hugged Emily back.

❖

Emily saw Andi pull into the driveway and opened the door before Andi had a chance to knock. "Hey there."

Andi cleared her throat. "Um, yeah, hi, I'm here to pick up my friend Emily. Is she here? Have you seen her?" She pretended to look down the hall, past Emily.

"Jerk." Emily grabbed Andi playfully by the collar and pulled her inside.

Emily had taken great pains in choosing her outfit and applying makeup. She did a little turn to give Andi a 360-degree view. After trying on at least a dozen outfits she'd decided on a tight, black, strapless dress that dipped down at the neckline enough to show a tease of cleavage without showing too much. A wide strip of shimmering gold material circled her waist. Emily thought it showed off the curve of her hips nicely. A gold chain around her neck with a delicate teardrop diamond and a pair of black pumps with the slightest bit of a heel finished the outfit perfectly.

"Wow, Emily. You look gorgeous."

"Thank you. I need to go touch up my makeup before we go."

"You don't need to. Really. You look great exactly like you are."

"Well, I am going to do it anyway. Come on in and make yourself comfortable. I'll only be a few minutes. You look pretty darn cute yourself, you know." *Beautiful, in fact.*

Andi wore a long-sleeved white button-down shirt with French cuffs. A thin leather belt looped around her waist, and her shirt was tucked neatly into black chinos. Crisp and clean, and yes, beautiful.

Emily touched up her lipstick and blush. She returned to find Andi and Mindy in the living room deep in a discussion about *I Love Lucy*. "And I pray for them every n-n-night." Mindy was saying. "God bless Lucy and Ricky and Fred and Ethel. I love them. Lucy is my best friend."

Andi smiled at the remark. And Emily silently smiled at Andi. Her heart swelled at the sight of her two favorite people.

"You do look really nice," Andi said, turning her attention to Emily. "Now go get your flannel shirt on so you don't freeze and we'll get going."

Emily chuckled. "I'm afraid my flannel shirt is at the cleaner's." She held up the black wrap she had in her hands. "I guess this will have to do." She brought it around her back and up to her shoulders, struggling to put it on straight.

Andi was on her feet in a split second. "Here, let me help." She untwisted the material in a single turn before gently draping it over Emily's shoulders and smoothing it out with her hands. Andi pressed her mouth against Emily's ear and whispered, "Are you sure you want to do this?"

Emily's stomach did a little flip and heat rose from her center. She swallowed hard against the feelings.

"Hey!" Mindy said loudly, startling both women. "You look bea-u-ti-ful, Emily."

"Thanks, honey," Emily said. "Anything you need before we go?"

Mindy shook her head. "Nope."

"Then I'll see you in a couple of hours. Okay? And don't stay up too late." Emily gave her little sister a squeeze before turning to Andi. "Ready?"

"Ready as I'll ever be, I guess."

CHAPTER TWELVE

A ndi had no trouble finding a parking spot in the large lot. "Here we are."

Emily wasn't sure what she was feeling. Excitement? Anxiety? Fear? Happiness? Yes. All of the above. She was so glad Andi was with her. She wouldn't have wanted anyone else by her side tonight. "Yep. Here we are."

Music thumped through the air and into Emily's chest as they entered the dimly lit bar. Small tables lined the wall next to a dance floor. A wraparound bar off to the left was almost completely filled with women. They seemed to be keeping the three female bartenders hopping. Another room beyond the dance floor held three pool tables and a few more tables and chairs.

"Where do you want to sit?" Andi said, right up next to Emily's ear.

The closeness made Emily's breath catch in her throat and sent a surge of electricity straight to her groin. Emily chose to ignore it.

"How about we sit there." Emily pointed to the tables near the wall. That whole section was raised a couple of steps higher than the rest of the place, and Emily thought she could observe the crowd better from that vantage point. Andi nodded, took Emily's arm, and led her up the steps. She pulled a chair out for Emily before sitting down opposite her.

A server was at the table within minutes to take drink orders. She looked like she was barely legal. Her purple glasses only added to her youthful appearance.

"I'll have a Seven and Seven. Thanks," Emily said, then turned her attention to the sights around her. It looked like a regular straight bar. The only thing different was the absence of men. She liked the difference.

Andi ordered a Coors Light from the tap when the server turned toward her.

"Anything to eat?" she asked them.

"Em?" Andi asked.

"What?" She was lost in sensory overload from the sights and sounds around her.

"Do you want anything to eat?"

Emily pulled her attention back to Andi. "No thanks." She was beginning to feel a bit overwhelmed but wasn't sure why. The feeling left her as soon as Andi smiled at her.

They sat in relative silence—well, except for the near-ear-splitting music coming through the sound system. The drinks arrived and Emily took a long swig. The couples on the dance floor slow danced to a song Emily didn't recognize. She was mesmerized by the swaying bodies. It was interesting how some of the dancers held each other with space between them, but most of the women were wrapped around each other as they moved in rhythm to the music. Emily noticed one couple wasn't dancing at all. The shorter of the two women was pressed up against the wall while her partner pressed into her, their mouths crushed together, almost frantically. Emily could see, even in the dim light, the woman against the wall squirming against the leg that her partner had pushed between her thighs. The sight made Emily's heart beat a little fast, and a small charge of electricity ran through her.

Pairs of women sat at the bar drinking and talking. Some exchanged kisses and subtle caresses. A few women sat alone nursing their drinks. Emily watched with fascination as an attractive redhead approached a brunette at the bar. The brunette swallowed the last of her drink and followed the redhead out on the dance floor. They stepped into each other's arms and slow danced, their bodies held close but without the familiar intimacy that she saw in some of the other dancers.

Emily smiled at Andi. "Wow. I've never experienced anything like this before. It's great."

"I'm glad you're enjoying yourself. Do you want another drink?"

She looked at the empty glass in her hand. She'd drained it without even realizing it. "Sure," Emily said. "Another Seven and Seven would be great."

Andi motioned the waitress over and ordered the drink for Emily. "You were pretty lost in your thoughts there."

"Sorry." Emily gave Andi a shy smile. "This is just so new to me. It only reaffirms what I want."

"Why?" Andi asked. "Is there someone here who interests you?" She scanned the crowd.

"No, I mean the whole thing. Seeing all these women together, dancing, laughing, kissing. I mean, it makes me want a woman in my life even more." Yes. This was what she wanted, what she had been missing her whole life. She looked out at the sea of possibilities before her. She glanced over at Andi, so glad she was here to share it with her.

Andi's eyes held an intensity that Emily hadn't seen before. Their eyes locked for a long moment. "I just want you to be happy, Em."

All Emily could do was nod. She was afraid that if she tried to speak in this moment, her emotions would overwhelm her and she would cry. Yes. This was it. She looked away and attempted to compose herself, feeling stupid for being so close to tears. They sat in silence as Emily finished her second drink, motioned the waitress over, and ordered another.

Emily was almost done with her third drink when Andi broke the silence and asked her if she wanted to play pool. "Sure," Emily said, glad for a diversion. "Can I get another drink?"

"Of course." Andi made a detour to the bar.

Emily leaned close to the bartender. "Whiskey sour," she said, loud enough to be heard over the music. "What would you like?" she asked Andi.

"Ginger ale," Andi half yelled back.

Emily paid for the drinks and handed the soda to Andi. They made their way to the pool tables. It was nice to get away from the thump of the music as they stepped into the room. It was quite a bit quieter.

Andi pumped quarters into the slots on the side of one of the pool tables. "Eight ball or straight pool?" she asked Emily, once she had the balls racked.

"Nothing straight tonight," Emily said, with a smile.

"Then eight ball it is." Andi took Emily's drink as she handed her a cue stick. She took a sip before setting it down on a table next to her ginger ale.

Emily leaned over to take a shot and thought she caught Andi checking out her cleavage as the weight of Emily's breasts pulled the black material of her dress down. Andi averted her eyes and Emily wasn't sure if she had been looking after all. She was disappointed that she might have, in fact, been mistaken. Disappointed? Disappointed that Andi might not have been checking her out? She considered it…Yes. Disappointed.

She shook the feeling away and hit the cue ball. The five ball landed squarely in the corner pocket. "Yes!" Emily said. "I get solids." She smiled at Andi and was rewarded with a big grin in return. Her breath caught in her throat for a moment. Andi looked even more beautiful when she smiled.

Distracted, she missed the next shot, and Emily reclaimed her drink while Andi took her turn, sinking three balls in a row. The glass was empty by the time Emily set it back down. She flagged down a waitress for another.

Several shots later, Andi was way ahead. "Eight ball, side pocket," she said. The cue ball slammed into the black ball and sent it flying. It slowed to a stop, but the cue ball continued on and sank out of sight into the pocket, winning Emily the game.

"Yes!" Emily exclaimed. "You scratched. I win."

Andi shook her head but couldn't seem to keep from smiling as Emily did a little victory dance. She picked up her empty glass and raised it in the air. "That deserves a little sex on the beach. Which is exactly what I want for my next drink." She ignored the fact that the room seemed to be spinning and everyone in it seemed a little off-kilter. "Can I have a Sex on the Beach?" Emily asked the waitress who had just entered the room. She managed to order the drink without giggling. She had no idea what was in it, but she liked the name. She set her empty glass down on the server's tray along with a twenty-dollar bill. "Andi, what would you like?" *Me? Would you like me? I'm thinking I'm a little drunk here. Andi would you like drunk me?* She laughed at her own thoughts and then pushed them away. Of course Andi wouldn't want her. That was just crazy. She and Andi were friends. Nothing more.

"Do you want to dance?" The question surprised Emily. It wasn't Andi asking. Why hadn't Andi asked her to dance?

Emily turned toward the voice. The woman resembled a young boy in her tan cargo pants, work boots, and red and black-checkered flannel shirt. Her short blond hair stood at attention in stiff spikes. Emily looked over at Andi, not sure what to say.

"Go ahead," Andi answered to Emily's unspoken question. There was that sense of disappointment again.

Emily accepted the stranger's extended hand and glanced at Andi over her shoulder as she was being pulled onto the dance floor. Andi was racking the pool balls, obviously planning on playing another round without Emily.

Emily felt a bit unsteady as the stranger pulled her into a soft embrace. Emily wasn't sure where she was supposed to put her hands, settling on the blonde's waist. After a few missed steps, Emily picked up the rhythm of the slow dance, and her movement flowed with her dance partner. It didn't feel quite natural, but Emily didn't know if that was because she was dancing with a woman or with someone she didn't know.

"Thanks," Emily said when the music faded. "I better get back to my friend."

"Thanks for the dance."

She peered toward the pool tables and saw Andi's backside bent over, pool stick in hand, getting ready to take a shot. Emily smiled sweetly, walked over to Andi, and pulled the cue stick from her hand just as she was bringing the stick back to hit the cue ball. She leaned the pool stick against the table and grabbed Andi by the hand.

"Dance with me," she said, and pulled Andi onto the dance floor, ignoring the surprised look on her face. Emily pulled Andi in close and wrapped both arms around her waist. They stepped into the rhythm of the music and each other effortlessly.

A sigh escaped from Andi's throat as Emily rested her head on her shoulder.

The warmth of the alcohol mixed with the warmth of Andi's body soothed Emily's soul. She closed her eyes and let the music carry her. It felt so right having Andi in her arms like this. Emily lifted her head and placed her cheek against Andi's. She knew it would only take a slight adjustment to have her lips on Andi's. It only took a second to make the decision *and* the adjustment. With her eyes still closed her lips brushed Andi's. But then the lips were gone and Emily felt nothing but air. She opened her eyes. The music played on, but their dancing had stopped.

Andi pulled her head back and out of the reach of Emily's mouth. "Emily, you've had a lot to drink. I don't think this is a good idea."

Emily's heart sank as the contents of her stomach threatened to rise. She reached for the right words to say. She needed to let Andi know how she felt. But she wasn't even sure herself exactly what that was. No words came to her. She felt light-headed and more than a little foolish. "I think it might be time to go home," she said.

"Are you all right?" Andi asked.

"I'm fine. You're right. I am not used to drinking that much. I'm sorry." But she wasn't sorry because she tried to kiss Andi. Just sorry Andi hadn't responded to the kiss. It was obvious that Andi wasn't having the same feelings she was.

"No, no, nothing to be sorry about. You're entitled to have a good time." Andi put her arm around Emily's shoulder and guided her out into the fresh air. They were silent on the ride home.

❖

Andi helped Emily out of the car and led her up the front step to her house. She took the key that Emily held out and unlocked the door. Once inside, Andi led her to her bedroom and sat her down on the bed. The fact that the room was spinning at a rapid rate and she had to hold on to the bed to keep from going with it told Emily she was definitely feeling the effects of the alcohol.

"Can you change your clothes by yourself?" Andi asked, as she pulled a T-shirt and sweatpants from Emily's dresser.

"I think so." Emily did her best to keep her words from slurring, concentrating on pronouncing the *th* clearly. She couldn't tell if she was successful or not. "I've been changing my clothes like a big girl since I was three." She giggled. "I need to check on Mindy first." She started to stand up, but the room took a sharp turn to the left and she sat back down to stop its motion.

"You change your clothes. I'll go check on Mindy." Andi closed the door behind her.

She was gone for only a minute or two. She knocked lightly on the door before entering Emily's room again.

"Who is it?" Emily said a little too loudly. She giggled again.

"Aren't you funny?" Andi said. "I thought you were going to change."

"I was trying." Emily realized that she had managed to put the T-shirt on—well, all but one arm—but hadn't touched the sweatpants. Her strapless black dress was crumpled on the floor. Andi picked it up and laid it neatly across the chair near the end of the bed, then helped Emily get the rest of the T-shirt on.

"I think I'm going to be sick." Emily did her best to stand up and get to the bathroom, but only managed to take one step. The vomit landed in heap at her feet. How she managed to miss herself and Andi, she didn't know. She didn't know whether to laugh or cry. The third option appeared to be to die from embarrassment.

Andi disappeared into the bathroom and returned with a towel and a wet washcloth. She eased Emily back onto the bed, watching where she stepped. The washcloth was warm as she wiped Emily's face and gently wiped it again with the towel. She placed the towel over the mess on the floor and returned to the bathroom, coming back with a glass of water and the bathroom trash can. She set the can by the bed.

"Drink this."

Emily took the glass and began to cry.

"Oh, honey, it's all right. You're okay." Andi rubbed a hand up and down her back.

The contact made Emily feel better. She sipped the water and did her best to hold back the remaining tears.

"It's right here if you want more." Andi set the glass of water on the nightstand. "Okay?"

Emily nodded.

"Can you stand for a second while I get the blankets moved?" Andi helped her to her feet and held her in place while she pulled back the blanket and bedspread. "Okay. Lie down."

Emily did as she was told.

"That's right." Andi pulled the blanket up around Emily. She cleaned up the mess on the hardwood floor using the towel and washcloth. She left again and returned with cleaning supplies to finish the job.

Emily watched her. "I'm sorry." A fresh round of tears rolled down her cheeks. "I only wanted us to have a good time."

Andi gave her a reassuring smile. "We did have a good time, right up till the puking part."

More tears. Andi's smile did little to make her feel less horrible.

"It's okay, Em. Honest." Andi brushed the hair from Emily's cheek and wiped her face again with a fresh washcloth. She leaned over and kissed Emily gently on the forehead before shutting off the light and leaving the room, this time leaving the door ajar.

Andi threw the towels and washcloths in the washer, added detergent, and turned it on. She checked on Mindy—sound asleep—and made herself comfortable on the couch. She thought back on the evening and the almost kiss, the kiss Andi wished she could have accepted. The kiss she would have accepted if Emily hadn't been drunk. But the last thing she wanted was to take advantage of Emily or have Emily hate her in the morning. Emily had just been caught up in the moment and the excitement of the evening. Andi was sure of it. If she wanted to keep Emily as a friend—and she did—she needed to be careful. Emily had said she wanted to explore this newfound life, and Andi was determined to let her. She would just have to stuff her feelings and her libido down. The last thing Emily needed was Andi being clingy or declaring her feelings. That would only confuse Emily, and Andi didn't want to risk having her pull away.

Andi tried to sleep but her brain wouldn't shut down. It replayed the evening again and again. Emily had pressed hard against her when they danced. The thought sent a surge of electricity though her. Emily's hair was soft under her fingertips, her scent fresh in her nose, her body… *Stop it! Just stop it.* This kind of thinking was getting her nowhere. She was going to make herself crazy.

She got up, switched the laundry from the washer to the dryer, and made herself a cup of tea. Plopping down on the couch again, she turned on the TV and flipped through the channels without really paying attention to what was on. Emily was sleeping in the other room. Emily. It would be so easy to slip in next to her. To hold her close and listen to her breathe. So easy.

CHAPTER THIRTEEN

A pounding head and what felt like a mouth full of cotton greeted Emily in the morning as she struggled to wake up. Fragments of memory from the night before skidded through her head, but some parts were a blank. She sat up trying to gather her senses. She realized that instead of her usual nightshirt, she had on a T-shirt and no bottoms. She noticed a pair of her sweatpants on the side of the bed and pulled them on.

Details from the previous evening began to creep in as she brushed her teeth in an attempt to lose the bad taste in her mouth. She rinsed her mouth with Scope and brushed her teeth again. *That's probably as good as it's going to get.* She had a vague memory of playing pool and dancing with Andi. *I must have had a very good time, seeing how bad I feel this morning.*

Taking medicine for her headache on an empty stomach might not be a good idea. *I wonder if toast would help ease this queasy stomach or make it worse.* She made her way toward the kitchen, almost in slow motion. She stuck her head in Mindy's room as she passed. Still sound asleep.

Emily was surprised to see Andi sleeping on the couch and tiptoed the rest of the way to the kitchen. She considered making a pot of coffee so it would be ready when Andi woke up but decided against it. She was sure the smell would make her sick. *Sick. Sick? I think I got sick last night. Oh my God, I think I threw up last night and Andi had to clean it. Oh. My. God.*

"How are you feeling?"

Emily jumped at the sound of Andi's voice. She turned toward her a little too fast and grabbed the counter for balance. "Andi. I am so sorry. I drank too much last night. That is so not me. I definitely don't drink like that."

"It's okay. You had a good time."

"How good a time? Did I get sick when I got home?"

"Just a little." Andi held up her hand, her thumb and finger about a half an inch apart. "Oh, that reminds me, you have some towels and washcloths in the dryer. I fell asleep before they were done."

"Andi, I'm so sorry. Really. Really sorry." She put her face in her hands.

"It's fine. So, how are you feeling?"

"Not too good. In fact, I think shitty would be a step up. You don't know any good hangover cures, do you?" Emily sat down at the table.

"I think there's one with raw eggs. Want some raw eggs?"

Emily held one hand over her mouth and the other in the air in front of her in an attempt to get Andi to stop. Not that she didn't deserve it.

"No, guess not. How about some Tylenol and dry toast, then?"

Emily nodded. "Thank you. There are pain meds in the cupboard next to the fridge."

Andi handed them to her with a glass of water.

"How come you're not hungover?" Emily asked after downing the pills.

"One of us had to stay sober to make sure you didn't get into any trouble. Besides, I didn't feel like taking a cab home." Andi made toast for Emily and put two more slices of bread into the toaster for herself.

"Oh damn. I didn't do anything stupid, did I?"

Andi leaned against the counter. "That depends on what you call stupid."

"What did I do? No. I don't want to know. What did I do?" Emily shook her head.

"No worries. I was there to look out for you."

"Thank you, Andi. I remember dancing. Did I dance with you? Did we dance?"

"We did."

Fragments of evening floated by but Emily couldn't quite capture them. She wanted to remember dancing with Andi. She wanted to remember what if felt like to have Andi's arms around her. "Maybe we can do that again sometime when I'm sober." Emily smiled despite the drum section playing in her head.

"I would like that very much."

CHAPTER FOURTEEN

D amn it, damn it, damn it." Emily couldn't decide what to wear. "How do I get myself into these things?" The sick feeling that rose up in her stomach was all too familiar. *Maybe I just won't go.*

Emily pulled two more blouses from her closet. She held them up in front her one at a time and looked in the full-length mirror. She threw both shirts on the large pile forming on the bed and went back to the closet to see what else she had to choose from. Seven shirts later she decided on a lavender blouse with black pants. It looked nice while still being casual. She decided against wearing her comfortable sneakers and slipped on a pair of black flats instead. A light application of makeup and a sweater completed the look.

❖

"Welcome, ladies, thank you for coming. I can tell already that we're going to have some fun here tonight. This is lesbian speed dating, so if you're looking for a man you are in the wrong place and should leave now." There were a few polite laughs at her stab at humor. The hostess—was that what she was called?—looked like she'd skipped a few too many meals. Her large, dangling earrings threatened to pull her over at any minute.

Emily looked around the poorly lit room. Soft music played

in the background as twenty or so women milled about. She was amazed by the different looks that the women sported. There were a couple of women that Emily would have thought were men if she saw them on the street. One woman wore a suit, complete with vest and tie, hair cut short and slicked back. A few women had on dresses and makeup. The rest of the women fell somewhere in between.

"Now, you were all given a number when you arrived. Does everyone have a card with their number?" There were murmurs all around. "Good," the hostess continued. She was way too perky or caffeinated. "Each table has two numbers on it. This tells you your starting place. You will have exactly three minutes to talk to the woman sitting across from you. When you hear this bell..." She held up a brass cowbell and rang it for all she was worth. Definitely overkill. "...if your number is an even number, for example, two, four, six and so on, you stay seated. If your number is an odd number, for example, one, three, five and so on, you move one table to your left. Does anyone *not* know if their number is an odd or even number?"

Oh, dear God. If anyone here doesn't know what an odd or even number is, I don't want to be dating them.

No one raised their hand. Several minutes and way too much instruction later, Emily grew impatient. She shifted her weight from one foot to the other and back again, willing the hostess to finish so they could get started.

"On the back of the card you are holding there is a list of numbers. You can choose yes or no for each number. If you wish to have further contact with any particular person, check the yes box next to their number. If not, check the no box. At the end of the evening, turn your cards in and you'll get an email tomorrow with the names and contact information of everyone that you had interest in that also had interest in you." She appeared to be out of steam after that long explanation. "Are there any questions?"

One hand went up, and everyone turned to look at a young woman with a bright pink streak down the center of her bleached blond hair. More disturbing than that were the five rings in her lower lip. Emily absently rubbed her own lip in the same spot.

"Um, yeah," pink-haired girl said. "What if we, like, want to get together with someone here, but they don't want to get together with us, so, like…is there like any way to get together with them if, you know, they don't have any interest in us? I mean, they really can't know us from three minutes, and if they had, like, five minutes, they might like us?"

Emily wondered how she could get that all out in one breath without passing out.

Pinky continued. "I have been to, like, literally a million of these things and I can't seem to meet the people I want to."

Emily smiled when she said *literally* and thought of Andi.

"Hmm, well, we can't give out any information to you if someone marks *no* on their card. Any other questions?"

Emily caught a glimpse of the number on the card the young woman was holding—eleven. Emily turned her card over and put a big *X* in the NO column next to that number.

Miss Perky held up the bell again. "Okay then, shall we get started? Everyone, please take your seats." She rang the bell and made a grand production out of pulling a stopwatch from her pants pocket.

Emily took her seat at the table with the number eight, corresponding to her card, on it. A moment later an attractive woman with dark blond hair that hung in soft curls around her face sat down across from her.

Okay. I can do this.

"And time staaaaarts now." The hostess rang the bell and pushed the start button on the stopwatch.

"She's a little obnoxious, isn't she?" number seven said.

Emily smiled. "Hi. I'm Emily."

"Tina."

"I'm an art teacher. What do you do?"

"I'm a nurse at Saint Joseph Hospital."

"Oh, that sounds interesting."

"It is. It's very interesting being a nurse."

"What kind of a nurse are you? I mean do you have a specialty?"

"Just general."

Emily searched her mind for questions. "Do you like it?"

"Yep."

Okay, so I could just sit and look at her. The hell with talking. This isn't as easy as I thought it would be. What else should I say? I need to get an actual conversation going here. We still have two and a half minutes left. "So, what do you like to do when you aren't working?" *That's a good question. We can talk about that.*

"Oh, not too much. I pretty much stay home with my cats."

"You have cats, huh? How many do you have?" Emily was determined.

"Six." Tina wasn't making this easy.

"Six? Wow, that's a lot of cats."

"I don't think so. My sister has ten."

Emily sighed and glanced at her watch. She couldn't believe how long three minutes was. She rested her chin on her hand and tapped her fingers on the table. "So why did you want to try speed dating?" *We'll try another approach.*

"To meet people...women...I like women."

"That makes sense. So, outside of teaching, I also paint in my spare time. Mostly oil paintings, but I also do some drawing."

"That's nice."

Emily wished that they had served something to drink. At least that way she could sip a glass of wine or play with the straw in her soda or dump a glass of milk on this woman's head just to liven things up. She couldn't help but giggle to herself at her thoughts. *Well, at least I can amuse myself.* She attempted one more try. "Sooooo..." *Oh, the hell with it.* They sat in silence until the bell rang.

Emily turned her card over and marked the number seven with an *X* in the NO column.

"Hi, I'm number nine." The next woman sat down and showed Emily her card as if she had to prove it.

"Nice to meet you, number nine. I'm Emily."

Number nine laughed. "Sorry, my name is Jennifer. Jenny." She reached across the table to shake Emily's hand. This conversation went much better than the first. Number nine was a legal secretary. She was out at work and her coworkers had no problem with her being gay. Her family also knew and, for the most part, were supportive, but her preacher brother wasn't happy about it. She avoided him whenever possible. She wasn't willing to give up family gatherings to avoid his rants. All in all, it was a good three minutes.

Number eleven, with the pink hair, sat down across from Emily. She talked and talked and talked. Emily wasn't sure what she was talking about, but it was fascinating watching those rings bounce up and down as her lips moved. The annoying cowbell clanged. *Thank God.*

The next woman seemed very attracted to Emily. Emily could tell by the number of times she said, "I'm very attracted to you, Emily," in the three-minute time frame. She also suggested several times that they leave "this joint, right now." Emily put yet another X in the NO column on the back of the card.

Most of the other women were a blur as they came and went. By the end of the evening, there were only two Xs in the YES column, Jenny and Belinda. Both had been easy to talk to and very easy on the eyes.

After turning her card in at the door, Emily headed out to her car, anxious to call Andi. Besides wanting to tell her how everything went, she just wanted to hear the sound of Andi's voice. It was exactly what she needed after such a nerve-racking evening.

CHAPTER FIFTEEN

Andi spread peanut butter on both slices of bread and stuck them together. Her phone sat on the counter next to her on speaker.

"Mindy's home. I rented her a movie and got her some snacks. She'll be fine. I don't plan on being out late."

Emily was sitting in her car outside of Loman's Restaurant.

"Do you want me to check on her?" Andi asked. It had been a week since Emily's speed dating evening and she was about to go on her first date with Jenny, the legal secretary.

Andi was doing her best to be a supportive friend. It wasn't easy. Emily had given her the complete rundown on the experience. Most of it sounded like a waste of time, but Emily had met a couple of women she was interested in, although Andi wasn't sure that three minutes of conversation gave Emily an opportunity to really get to know someone.

"If you're bored, you can give her a call. But she's okay alone for a while. Listen, I have to get going, I don't want to be late. I'll call you when I get home. Bye. And, Andi? Thanks."

"You're welcome," Andi said, knowing that Emily had already hung up. "It's the least I can do for my best friend—who I secretly have feelings for."

She took her sandwich into the living room and sat down just as Butch jumped up on the couch beside her. She gave the cat a quick scratch behind her ears and was rewarded with a loud purr. "So, here's the story," she said to the cat. "Emily's going out on a date, and I don't want her to." Butch turned around a couple of times and settled in next to Andi. "Does that make me a bad friend? Should I tell her I like her? I mean like *really* like her?"

Butch didn't answer.

"I'll take that as a no. You're right. We've been through this. If she had similar feelings, I would know it. Obviously she doesn't. The only time I thought maybe she did, she was drunk and she never attempted to kiss me after that when she was sober."

Butch licked her paw and proceeded to run it over her head, cleaning herself.

Andi was undeterred by the feline's lack of interest. "She is too busy meeting new people and having a gay old time. See what I did there? A gay old time. Get it?"

She took a bite of her sandwich and chewed slowly, not really feeling like eating after all.

❖

Emily walked into the small restaurant and looked around. She hoped she would recognize Jenny when she saw her. She didn't have to worry because Jenny recognized her and came right over and gave a shy hug.

"Nice to see you again," Jenny said.

"You too."

"I have a table already. I hope that's okay."

"Certainly. Lead the way." Antique tools and toys hung from the dark rustic walls in random groups scattered about. The fireplace in the corner added to the cozy feeling, and Emily could smell the real wood fire as it burned. Too many places used gas fireplaces these days, and Emily had never been fond of them. She followed Jenny to a small table in the corner.

Emily looked through the menu. She made her decision pretty quick and set the menu down.

"What are you going to have?" Jenny asked.

"I was thinking a turkey burger and fries," Emily answered.

"Oh, are you a vegetarian?"

What? Emily scratched her head. *Oh my God, wait till I tell Andi this one. To the best of my knowledge, a turkey isn't a vegetable.* She did her best to suppress a giggle. "No. I love animals but have no problem eating a good steak or turkey burger now and then." Emily smiled, but Jenny didn't. *Uh-oh. Wonder if I offended her.* "Are you a vegetarian?"

"No. I just don't eat fowl." She gave Emily a small smile. It seemed forced.

"You're a legal secretary, right?" Time for small talk and change of subject.

"Yes. I've worked for Binder and Miles downtown for about six years now. I really like it. I love the law."

"I got called for jury duty last year but didn't have to serve because I walked in and yelled, 'let my people go.'"

Nothing. No laugh or even a smile from Jenny.

"I'm kidding. I did my civic duty and served on the jury."

"Good. I think it's an important thing to do."

"I agree. We need to do the right thing in life."

The waiter arrived order pad in hand. "Are you ready to order?" He had an easy smile and a gap between his top front teeth.

"We are. Go ahead, Jenny."

"I'll have the garden salad with Italian dressing and a Diet Coke," Jenny said.

"And for you, miss?" the waiter asked Emily.

"Can I get a turkey burger, fries well done, and a glass of water with lemon, please?" She handed her menu to him. "Thank you," she looked at his name tag, "Kevin."

He nodded, took Jenny's menu, and was gone.

"My friend Andi told me this was a great place to eat. I recently moved here from Rochester, so I don't know a lot about Syracuse yet."

"Oh. How come you moved?" Jenny unfolded her napkin and neatly placed it on her lap.

"I was running from the law." No reaction. *She isn't getting my humor.* "I'm kidding. I got a teaching job here."

Having a relationship with anyone that didn't get her humor was out of the question. "What would you say if I offered you a kidney?" She was trying to keep herself amused now, knowing this was going nowhere.

"What? Why would you do that?" The edge to Jenny's voice was unmistakable.

"I wouldn't. Just me being silly. Silly me." She said the last part under her breath.

Emily did her best to enjoy the evening but all in all found it pretty boring. They split the bill at the end of the meal and neither mentioned a second date. That was all right with Emily. She had no interest in seeing Jenny again. There had to be more interesting women out there. Emily was determined to find them.

❖

Mindy was already in bed, watching the small TV Emily had bought for her. "How was the movie I got for you?" Emily sat down on the side of the bed.

"Great. Shrek is my best friend. How was your d-d-dinner?"

"The food was good."

"Did you have fun?"

"No, but that's okay. It was a learning experience. I'm going to go get ready for bed. Don't stay up too late. I'll see you in the morning." Emily kissed the top of Mindy's head.

"Good night, Emily."

Emily went into her room and closed the door. She sat on her bed and called Andi. "Hi, it's me."

"Hey. How was your evening?" Andi asked.

"Her head didn't spin around or anything like that."

"So is that good or bad?"

"It would have been really bad if her head spun around, so I guess it was…no, wait. Now that I think about it, it would have been a step up if her head had spun around. At least that would have entertained me. The evening was very boring."

"I'm sorry, Em. Personally, I hate when I am on a date with someone and her head spins around. It always scares me, 'cause it's usually followed by green stuff pouring out of her mouth."

Emily laughed. "This is what was missing," Emily said. "Humor. A connection. A personality."

"She had no personality?"

"She was nice enough but she had no sense of humor—and apparently she thinks that turkey is a vegetable." Emily tried to stifle a giggle.

"Do I even want to know what that means?"

Emily relayed the story and other details of the night. They were both laughing hysterically by the time they hung up the phone.

Emily always felt better after talking to Andi. She was so lucky to have her. She set the phone on the nightstand and went to take a shower. The hot water felt good on her skin and she leaned her head back farther under the spray. An image of Andi in the shower with her flashed through her mind. Andi's lips were on her exposed neck. Her body reacted with a surge of moisture. *Wow. Where did that come from?* She tried to push the thought aside, but the feeling in her body remained. Emily adjusted the faucet to cool the water down. But it did little to cool the fire she was feeling inside. *What the hell?* This sort of thing seemed to be happening more and more when she was near Andi or merely thought of her. Maybe her body was trying to tell her something. She wasn't sure she was ready to listen. She wasn't sure she wanted to risk the friendship. Was she?

Chapter Sixteen

Andi and Emily ran to Andi's house just as the sky opened up and it started to pour. Andi sprinted ahead and unlocked the door. She pushed it open and stepped in as Emily reached the house.

"That was close. I almost got wet." Andi said, panting.

"A little rain won't hurt you." Emily bumped Andi's shoulder with her own. She wiped a drip of rainwater as it ran down from her forehead.

"Oh yeah, it would. I could melt."

"Like the Wicked Witch?"

"No! Not like the Wicked Witch. More like I'm made out of sugar."

"You're made out of sugar all right." Emily laughed as she sat, sinking down into the overstuffed chair.

"This isn't funny, Emily. I *am* made out of sugar and I'll melt, I tell ya. When I was younger I had some water spill on my leg, and now I am all deformed where my sugar leg melted."

"Prove it. Let me see." Emily was half hoping Andi would bare her naked leg.

Andi sat down in the rocking chair across from Emily. "You want to see my deformed leg? Is that what you're saying? It isn't pretty, Emily."

"I'm having trouble believing this story of yours, especially since you won't show me the evidence."

"I am not going to show you my leg. I don't care how much you beg."

"Okay, okay. Don't show me your leg. I didn't want to see it anyway." Emily suppressed her laughter. "Hmm, want to get into your hot tub with me?"

Andi feigned a shocked look. "Are you trying to kill me, woman?"

The sound of laughter filled the room as both women broke into hysterical giggling.

Andi wiped tears from her cheeks. "Let's do it."

"Do what?" Emily asked.

"Let's go in the hot tub. It'll be great. It sounds like the rain is slowing down, and it'll take the chill off. Besides, the roof overhang will protect us."

"I didn't bring a bathing suit, and besides, I thought you would melt."

"I was just funning ya on the melting stuff. Come on, I'm sure I have a suit you can wear—or you can go in naked."

Emily put her finger on her chin and looked up toward the ceiling. "Hmm, let me think about it. Um, no, I don't think so. Don't think I will be getting naked in the hot tub."

"Then let's go see what I have for bathing suits." Andi stood up. She grabbed Emily's hand and dragged her into the bedroom.

Emily had never been in Andi's bedroom before. The warm blue walls were glazed with a glossy dark blue that matched the trim around the windows and doorframe. "This is beautiful," Emily said. "Who did you get to paint this for you?"

"I did it myself," Andi said.

"You did a wonderful job. I love it." Emily's attention was drawn to the queen-sized bed. "And who made the quilt?" She pushed an image of Andi lying across the bed from her mind and tried to concentrate on the pattern.

"My grandmother made that for me. Isn't it great?" Andi ran her hand over the quilt lovingly. "The pattern's called Friendship

Garden. Some of the fabric pieces were taken from my baby clothes. The yellow material in the center of each block is from my first baby blanket. And this one," she said, pointing to a pink floral fabric, "is a maternity shirt that my mother wore when she was pregnant with me."

"Oh Andi, it's beautiful." Emily's eyes met Andi's and held for several moments. Emily looked away, suddenly realizing that what she wanted more than anything else in that moment was for Andi to kiss her. She pretended to be interested in the collection of tiny dolls lined up on the top of the dresser. It was beginning to feel too warm in Andi's bedroom.

"Most of those were gifts from my mom. I guess she figured if I could get interested in *girly* things like dolls it might turn me straight." Andi's voice brought her out of her own thoughts—almost.

"You're kidding."

"Nope. It's the truth. She hasn't given me one in a few years, so I'm thinking she's given up. Funny thing is, I like the dolls. Some of them are collector's items." Andi pulled open the top drawer of the dresser. "Here you go. Bathing suits. Take a look and see if there's anything you want to wear."

Emily pulled a black one-piece bathing suit with small gold rings that connected the material together at the hips. A quick peek at the label also told Emily that it should fit. "How about this one?" she asked.

"What a lovely choice," Andi said with a smile. "Go ahead and change in my bathroom there and I'll change in the bathroom down the hall. I'll meet you at the back door with towels."

Andi pawed through the other suits while Emily went to change.

Alone in the bathroom Emily took a few moments to gather her thoughts and tell herself how ridiculous she was being. She took her time undressing, carefully folding her clothes and setting them on the closed toilet seat. She eased the suit up over her butt and hips, taking a quick look at her legs, glad that she shaved them that morning. The bathing suit fit snugly, but not too tight that it was uncomfortable. She attempted to close the clasp that held the suit together behind her neck but couldn't seem to get it to work. It worked perfectly fine when she pulled the straps down and tested it. She tried once again to fasten behind her neck. No luck. Holding the two pieces firmly in place she set out looking for Andi's help.

Andi hadn't come out of the other bathroom yet. Emily, in an attempt to lighten her mood, tiptoed over to the closed door and leaned against the jamb, her face inches from the door. She waited. Her plan was to yell "Boo" as soon as Andi opened the door.

It was only a matter of seconds before the door flew open and Andi stepped out, directly into Emily. Emily wasn't prepared for Andi to come out so quickly. Or so forcefully. Both women were startled by the sudden appearance of the other. Instead of yelling "Boo" as planned, Emily dropped the straps to the bathing suit, causing the front of the suit to drop down as Andi stepped into her. Andi's arms came out in front of her in an attempt to keep her balance. She ended up with her arms wrapped around Emily. It stopped Emily from falling backward out of the bathroom doorway and sent a rush of electricity through her at the skin-to-skin contact.

"What the hell are you doing?" Andi asked as she burst out laughing.

"Scaring you." Emily looked up into Andi's eyes. Deep eyes. Brown eyes. Beautiful eyes. She swallowed hard and then joined in the laughter.

Andi started to release Emily from her grip when Emily's arms went around Andi and held her tightly, preventing her from stepping back. Emily's heart beat wildly. She wasn't sure if it was the close contact with Andi or embarrassment from the fact that the top of her bathing suit had fallen and was down around her waist.

Andi looked into Emily's eyes in an apparent attempt to read them. "What are we doing?"

"Not what you think." Emily could feel the heat inside her rising. "My top fell down and I'm trying to keep myself covered...um...with your body."

Andi put her arms around Emily again. "Okay."

Andi's breath on her face sent a tingle down Emily's spine and goosebumps erupted across her skin.

"What do you want to do about this?" Andi's face radiated warmth as a blush traveled up her neck to her face.

"How about you close your eyes and I turn around and pull my top up?" Emily suggested.

"Okay, you got it." Andi closed her eyes.

"Andi?"

"Yes?" Andi said, eyes still closed.

"You need to let me go."

Andi opened her eyes. "What?" Her arms were still tightly wrapped around Emily. "Oh sorry." She closed her eyes again and released her.

Emily took a step back and spun around pulling up her top in the process. "Okay, you can open your eyes now." Emily held the suit's material tight against her chest. "Would you mind helping me with this?"

Andi fastened the straps together. She set her hands on Emily's bare shoulders when she finished. "All set."

Emily closed her eyes, soaking in the feeling of Andi's warm hands on her. She took a deep breath before opening them again and turning around. The sight in front of her made her breath stop altogether. Andi's deep blue bathing suit hugged her body like a second skin. The sides were cut away, showing the curve and soft skin above her hips. The top was cut low and Andi's breasts pushed upward, adding to their fullness.

Emily forced her eyes from Andi's chest to her face. She cleared her throat. "I'm ready whenever you are. Do you have the towels?"

"I'll get them." Andi pulled two towels from the hall closet and handed one to Emily. Out on the deck, they removed the hot tub cover and set it aside. Andi slipped into the tub in one quick movement.

Emily sat on the edge of the tub, swung her legs over the side, and let her body slide into the hot water. She settled down next to Andi. The tension left her body as the hot water surrounded her. The strong jets forced water and bubbles toward her and dimpled her skin where they hit.

The rain had stopped and steam rose from the hot tub into the cool, damp mid-October air. "I don't see that you're melting." Emily tapped Andi's knee. "And I didn't see any deformities on your legs either."

"You were looking at my legs?"

"No. I wasn't looking at your legs. I was just looking and your legs happened to be in my line of vision."

"I keep my deformities hidden. You can't see them, but I know they're there."

The conversation took a serious turn for a moment. "I guess to some extent we all keep our deformities hidden." Emily paused, choosing her words carefully. "Sometimes I wonder if Mindy has an advantage or a disadvantage because her"—Emily did air quotes with her fingers—"'deformity' is there for all the world to see. She doesn't get to hide it, like the rest of us."

"Do you have deformities?" Andi asked quietly. "Because, Emily Sanders, you seem perfect to me."

The two women looked at each other for what seemed like hours but was only seconds as the water swirled around them. Emily leaned toward Andi without breaking eye contact and ran her hand swiftly through the water, her palm leading the way, causing a large splash of water to hit Andi in the face. She needed to do something to keep herself from kissing Andi full on the mouth. Splashing water seemed like the perfect solution.

"Hey! No roughhousing in the hot tub," Andi said as she sent a wall of water back at Emily.

Emily laughed as the water dripped from her hair and she wiped it away from her eyes.

The laughter died away as the women once again relaxed into the water. Emily closed her eyes. The only sound in the air was the bubbles in the water coming to the surface and the hum of the hot tub motor.

Emily was very aware of just how close Andi was to her. Their shoulders rested against each other, skin touching skin. She felt flushed from the contact. The heat she felt was coming from more than just the water. "I certainly hid being gay," Emily said, cutting through the silence, her eyes still closed. "Not that I'm calling that a deformity. But I hid it so well that even I didn't see it. Sometimes common sense eludes me. I think *that* is one of my deformities. I can't see what is right in front of me." After several seconds she asked, "Do you think that makes me stupid or blind?"

"Oh, Emily. That makes you human."

"Being human is hard sometimes."

"It sure is. But it's also great most of the time."

Emily opened one eye and glanced at Andi. Andi's eyes were closed. Tiny beads of sweat formed on her upper lip. Emily resisted the urge to run her finger across it. *It sure is great most of the time. And confusing. And...and...and...*

Andi opened her eyes. "Whatcha doing?"

Emily's blush added to the heat of the water. She just smiled and shook her head.

"You're hot."

"What?" Emily opened her eyes.

"Hot. Too hot. Your face is looking a little red. You can't stay in the hot tub too long 'cause you can get too hot and it fries your brains. So, we need to get out before our brains fry."

"Seriously?"

"Well, our brains won't actually fry—I think. But yeah, you shouldn't stay in for too long."

Emily rose and eased out of the tub. The cool air felt good

against her hot skin. She grabbed the towels from the deck railing and waited while Andi got out. She watched as a drop of water ran from Andi's chin, down her long neck, and over her chest, coming to rest on the swell of flesh before descending and being lost in the cloth of Andi's bathing suit. Emily realized she was staring and turned her eyes away as she handed Andi her towel. She was in no hurry to dry herself, hoping the cool air would quell the heat that was rising in her. The heat continued despite the air, and she wrapped the large towel around her, slid open the glass door, and stepped into the house. She left the door open for Andi to follow but didn't wait for her to come in before going into Andi's bathroom to change her clothes.

She emerged several minutes later fully dressed, towel and wet bathing suit in hand. Andi was nowhere in sight and the sliding glass door was closed, so Emily assumed Andi was changing in the other bathroom. She deposited the wet items in the plastic basket on top of the washer in the laundry room and barely avoided running into Andi as Andi entered the room with her own wet things.

"Hi," Andi said.

"Hi," Emily said back.

"Would you like something to drink?"

"No, I think I am going to stay away from alcohol for a little while," Emily said.

"I was thinking more like water. It's a really good idea to drink water after you get out of the hot tub. Go make yourself comfortable in the living room and I'll get us some."

Emily sat in the rocking chair and pushed off the floor with her toes setting the chair in motion. She needed to use up some of the extra energy coursing through her. Sexual energy? She didn't know.

"Thanks." Emily took the water Andi held out but avoided looking at her. She didn't trust what she was feeling. She drank half of the water down in one long swig. "I think I'm going to get going after I finish my water." She needed to get away, think about things. Because what she really wanted to do was to be as close to Andi as possible.

Andi walked her to the door and gave her a tight hug. "I had a great day. Thanks so much for the pleasure of your company."

"It was a pleasure giving you pleasure," Emily said without thinking. "Um. I mean I enjoyed it too. I'll see you at school tomorrow. Don't forget you're coming over to watch movies on Friday night."

"I won't forget. I'll see you tomorrow. Have a good night."

Andi leaned against the open door and Emily knew she was watching her as she walked to her car. She gave a quick wave and backed out of the driveway. Yes. She needed to put space between them before she did something stupid. Because what she really wanted right now was to do something stupid.

CHAPTER SEVENTEEN

"Oh my God. You look terrible," Andi said, when Emily opened the door. "You're so pale." *But still beautiful. Always beautiful.*

"Gee, thanks. I was hoping I would feel better by the time you got here. Guess my plan didn't work. There's a twenty-four-hour bug going around at school. I'm sure that's what I have. I was hoping to get rid of it in more like four hours."

"No such luck, huh?"

"Nope."

Andi put her hand up to Emily's forehead. "You feel warm. I think you've got a fever. Did you take anything? Aspirin or anything?"

Emily shook her head. "We can cancel if you want. I should have. But I really wanted to spend time with you."

The sentiment went straight to Andi's heart. She felt the same way. Sick or not, she wanted to be with Emily. She welcomed the opportunity to take care of her. She deposited Emily on the couch, went to fetch some Tylenol and water, and handed them to Emily.

"Where's Mindy?"

"She is spending the night at Daisy's house."

"We don't have to watch a movie if you feel sick. I'll sit with you for a while if you want me to." Andi hoped she would let her stay.

"I would love that." Emily mustered up a smile.

Andi sat down next to her and leaned back. "Come here and lay your poor, sick head on my bosom."

Emily looked at her and smirked. "What kind of a person uses the word 'bosom'?"

Andi feigned offense. "Apparently a person who spent way too much time with their grandmother as a kid."

"I don't want to get you sick."

"I'm not worried about it. If I get sick, I know you'll take care of me." She knew it was true.

"You bet your sweet ass I would."

"I knew you thought my ass was sweet."

"Actually I thought you were more of a smartass than a sweet ass. But I'm starting to change my mind." Emily leaned into Andi, settling her head more on her lap than on her *bosom*. "Thank you."

Andi pulled the blanket from the back of the couch and covered Emily with it. "How's that?"

Emily let out a contented sigh. "It's perfect. You're perfect."

"I know." Andi stroked her shoulder.

Emily snuggled in closer. "I don't feel so good," Emily said.

"I know, baby. I'm here. I'll take care of you."

"I was going to make us popcorn and we were supposed to have a nice night watching movies. I even got one with girl-on-girl action, just for you."

Andi could hear the smile in Emily's voice, even though she couldn't see her face. "Shh, we can watch them another time. You rest now."

"Tell me more about your grandmother."

"My grandmother, huh? Well, let's see. She's about four foot nothing, round, and happy. I loved spending time with her as a kid. She makes the best tomato sauce you've ever eaten and she always smells a little bit like garlic. She told me never to swallow my gum because my guts would stick together. You don't get better advice than that. She loves to read and travel and really live. She loves me and I love her."

"Uh-huh," Emily said, so low Andi could barely hear it.

"She's going to love you too, when she gets to meet you. She'll know just how special you are." Andi gently brushed her fingers through Emily's hair. *And you are special, my friend. Very special.*

"Andreina," Emily whispered, and drifted off to sleep.

Andi let out a contented sigh.

CHAPTER EIGHTEEN

Emily awoke to a rhythmic sound coming from right behind her. Confused, she opened her eyes and blinked a few times. It took several moments for her to get her bearings. There was sunlight streaming in through the windows and she realized she was in the living room. The details of last night drifted back to her through her morning haze. That rhythmic sound was Andi breathing.

Emily was lying on her side, her head across Andi's lap. Andi's hand was resting on Emily's waist, skin touching skin. Heat radiated from it, but Emily didn't know if it was from Andi's hand or the reaction her own flesh had to Andi's sleeping touch.

"Andi," Emily said softly. "Andi," she said a little louder. "Andi!"

"Huh?" Andi was awake now but not fully articulate.

Emily rolled over onto her back and looked up at Andi. The movement caused Andi's hand to travel from her waist to her stomach and Emily felt heat in the pit of her stomach and below.

"Are you awake?"

"Huh? Um, yeah. How are you feeling?" She looked down at Emily and smiled. Her hand absently caressed Emily's stomach.

Emily's breath caught in her throat.

Andi pulled her hand away and rubbed her eyes.

Emily felt the loss of Andi's touch immediately. "I'm feeling much better. But I bet you feel sore as hell from sleeping in that position."

"I'm okay," Andi tilted her head, stretching her neck muscles, first one way and then the other.

Emily felt both a little awkward and a little turned on with her head on Andi's lap, looking up at her. "How about you go take a shower and I'll make us something to eat?" She sat up reluctantly, not really wanted to leave the position she had been in.

"Are you sure you're up to it? You weren't feeling too great last night."

"I'm sure. A hot shower will do you good." She reached across the short distance between them and rubbed Andi's knee. "Thank you for taking care of me last night."

"My pleasure," Andi answered, with a shy smile. "And I think I will go take a shower."

Emily rose from the couch, grabbed Andi's hands, and pulled her to her feet.

"Good. Use my bathroom. The towels are in the cabinet, shampoo is in the shower. Feel free to look through my drawers to find something to wear." Emily turned Andi around by the shoulders. She resisted the urge to pat her on the butt and instead patted her on the back and said, "Now go." She didn't, however, resist the urge to watch Andi's rear end as she walked away.

The smell of bacon and coffee filled the air as Emily put the final touches on breakfast. Andi appeared right on time, donning a pair of Emily's jeans and a T-shirt and no bra. Emily could see her nipples poking through the thin material. She was barefoot. *Sexy.* Emily pushed the thought away. "Those clothes fit you great."

"I even managed to get into your pants." Andi blushed, obviously realizing how that sounded.

Emily laughed. "You wish." But she was beginning to wonder just who was wishing what. "Come on and sit down."

Andi sat. "I appreciate your making me breakfast."

Emily set a cup of coffee down in front her. She really did look good in her clothes. "And I appreciate you staying with me last night. Having you here really did make me feel so much better."

"Anytime. Let me know whenever you need me to spend the night with you."

The innocent statement sent a surge through Emily. The thought of spending the night with Andi in her bed made her whole body go hot. She set about the task of buttering toast with her back to Andi in an attempt to hide her feelings and sort through her thoughts.

"Are you all right?" Andi's voice startled her.

"Yep," Emily answered, her back still to Andi. She spooned the scrambled eggs from the pan on the stove into a bowl.

"You're just very quiet all of a sudden. Does your head still hurt?"

Emily turned around and attempted a smile. "My head is fine. Although I guess that's a matter of opinion."

"Well, if my opinion counts, your head is more than fine."

"In that case, yes. Your opinion does count. Thanks." Emily wondered if Andi was having any of the same feelings. She wasn't even sure what feelings she was having and told herself to figure out her own thoughts and feelings before trying to figure out someone else's.

CHAPTER NINETEEN

Emily was a little more than surprised on Wednesday when Belinda called to see if she was interested in going out for a drink on Saturday night. Emily had all but forgotten about her. Belinda was the only other person besides Jenny whom Emily had met on her speed dating adventure that she had had the slightest bit of interest in. That had been nearly a month ago.

Emily hesitated before answering. The date with Jenny hadn't gone too well, and Emily was trying to sort out her feelings for Andi. She didn't know if she wanted to go out with Belinda after all.

"It's just a drink," Belinda said, after getting no response. "Or how about coffee Saturday afternoon? No pressure. I'd like the opportunity to get to know you a little better."

"Sure," Emily said at last. *What would be the harm in having coffee?* "Where and what time?"

"Which are you saying yes to? The drink or the coffee?"

"The coffee, if that's okay with you," Emily said.

"That's fine." Belinda proceeded to give her the information and directions. "I look forward to seeing you again."

"Me too," Emily said, but she wasn't sure she meant it.

❖

The crisp feeling of fall permeated the air as Emily walked across the parking lot. The sun was shining, but the blowing wind negated any warming effect it might have had. She pulled the collar of her fleece jacket up higher to shield her neck. Many of Emily's friends considered this a great time of year. They loved the changing colors of the leaves and the escape from the heat of summer. Emily couldn't understand that. To her, the gold and orange leaves meant that the cold of winter would soon be settling in. She didn't like the cold and she knew that Syracuse, like Rochester, could get pretty darn cold in the winter.

She had chosen the house she bought in North Syracuse not only because of the large windows in the den that became her studio but also because it had that wonderful fireplace. She pictured the fireplace stacked with seasoned wood ablaze with a warm crackling fire. The image included a glass of wine in her hand and Andi softly kissing her neck. She closed her eyes for a moment and stopped walking. She shook her head to dislodge the image from her mind.

"Jeez," she said under her breath. *Here I am meeting someone for coffee—okay, let's get real here—meeting someone for a date, and I'm thinking about Andi kissing me? That is so not cool. What kind of a person am I?*

She shook her head again and walked the rest of the way to the door. She could smell the fresh coffee as soon as she pushed it open. She walked to the counter and waited as an elderly man paid his bill.

"Table for one?" the hostess asked her as she handed the man his change.

"No, I'm supposed to meet someone. Her name is Belinda. Would you happen to know if she's here yet?" Emily looked around to see if she could see her, not a hundred percent sure she would recognize her.

"Emily?" She turned at the sound of her name. Belinda had come in behind her. She was prettier than Emily remembered. Her ash-blond hair was cut short and tapered around her face.

Her dark eyes were bright against her pale skin. The tan trench coat she wore was tied loosely at the waist with a matching belt.

"Yes." Emily smiled. "Here she is," Emily said to the hostess. "Table for two, please."

"Right this way." The hostess grabbed two menus from under the counter. Emily and Belinda followed her into the dining area.

Belinda removed her overcoat, revealing a dark red turtleneck sweater and black pleated skirt. She looked nice. Emily wondered if she was underdressed in her best jeans and casual white blouse.

The waiter appeared with a pot of coffee. "Yes," both women answered in unison when he asked if they wanted any.

He filled both cups. "I'll be back in a few minutes for your orders, ladies."

Emily poured her usual amount of half-and-half and sugar into her cup and stirred it while Belinda watched with amusement.

"A little coffee and a lot of cream and sugar, huh?" Belinda said.

Her statement brought Emily back to the first time she had coffee with Andi.

"I wasn't sure you still wanted to get together when I called you."

"I wasn't sure either," Emily said honestly.

"And yet here we are. Why?"

Emily studied Belinda, trying to decide how much to tell her. "Hmm, well, I guess I wasn't sure if I wanted to go out with you. Nothing personal, nothing against you, I'm sure you're a great person."

"I am," Belinda said with a smile. "So why the hesitation?"

"Because I'm pretty sure I'm falling in love with my best friend." *There.* Emily closed her eyes for a moment. *I said it. I said it out loud.* She repeated it. "I think I'm falling in love with my best friend."

"I'm thinking this might get in the way of our dating,"

Belinda said. "I'm joking. I'm sorry. I'm a good listener if you want someone to talk to. I'm getting the feeling that you've been keeping this all bottled up. Does your friend know?"

"I'm the one who's sorry. What a thing to tell you on our first date." Emily could feel her face turn red.

"Under the circumstances, let's not think of this as a first date. Let's think of it as two friends having coffee together." She gave Emily a reassuring look.

"I would really appreciate that. I haven't talked to anyone about this. But I don't think it would be very fair of me to dump all this on you."

"It's fine. Truly, it is." She reached across the table and gave Emily's hand a quick squeeze. "Honest."

"No, I haven't told her how I feel."

"Why not?"

"I'm not sure how she feels about me."

"How are you ever going to find out if you don't tell her?"

"I guess I'm afraid of losing her if I tell her and she doesn't feel the same."

The waiter reappeared at the table. "All set to order?"

"I think I'm going to stick to the coffee," Emily said peering up at him. She turned to Belinda. "But you go ahead and order something to eat. Don't let me stop you."

"Just the coffee for me too," Belinda said to the waiter. When he left she said to Emily, "She hasn't given you any indication of how she feels? Do you even know if she's gay?"

"That's the only part I am sure of."

"Is she seeing anyone else?" Belinda asked.

"No. I thought she was and felt hurt and, I think, a little jealous, but I wasn't sure of my feelings at that point. I wasn't even sure I was gay then."

"So these are pretty new feelings for you?"

Emily told Belinda about Sarah and her recent self-revelations. Of course, she skipped over some of the more personal and embarrassing details. Three cups of coffee later they were still deep in conversation.

"I guess the bottom line here is that I don't know what to do with these feelings."

"That's quite a bottom line."

"What should I do?"

"Oh, Emily, I can't tell you what to do. I think you need to listen to your heart."

CHAPTER TWENTY

I know it's late notice, but would you like to come over for lunch today? I've hardly seen you at all this week," Andi asked Emily over the phone on Sunday morning. "Bring Mindy too."

"I can come but Mindy has plans with friends."

"Hmm, okay, I guess you can come without Mindy."

"Gee, thanks. What can I bring?"

"Just your lovely self. About one o'clock?"

"One o'clock works for me. I'll see you then. Bye." Emily hit the End button on her cell phone and tapped it against her chin. "And maybe I'll tell you I have feelings for you today." Emily closed her eyes and shook her head. "Or maybe not."

❖

"Hey there, come on in." Andi stepped back, letting Emily pass. "You look nice."

I could brush against her breasts as I walk by her, Emily thought as she came through the door. *See if she likes it or pushes me away.* "Hi," she said instead. She was feeling unusually unsure of herself today.

"What's new?" Andi led the way into the kitchen.

"Not much." *If you don't count the fact that after thirty-five years of life I figured out I was gay, and it only took me a few more weeks to realize I want to be with you.* Emily wanted to kick herself in the head to get her brain to stop the stupid thoughts and sarcastic remarks. "How about with you? Anything new going on?"

"No, but I've been a little worried about you." Andi pulled out a chair for Emily and then sat down next to her. "I've hardly seen you this week, and when I do, you don't seem like yourself. So, tell me what's going on."

"I've just been a little off this week."

Andi tilted her head and raised her eyebrows.

"Really, I'm fine," Emily said.

Andi took both of Emily's hands in her own. "Would you tell me if you weren't?"

Emily looked down at her hands in Andi's. For a moment she felt like she might cry. She looked up and into the face of the woman she considered her best friend. She was sure of her feelings now. She wanted Andi, and she was scared of Andi not wanting her back. She was scared of losing Andi. She wasn't sure she should tell her. "Yes. I would tell you if something was wrong." *But I'm not sure I can tell you that something is right.*

"Okay." Andi let go of her hands and stood up. She leaned over and kissed Emily on the cheek. Emily closed her eyes and willed herself not to turn her head to meet Andi's lips.

"I hope soup and sandwiches are okay. I thought it would be nice on a chilly day like this." Andi grabbed a loaf of bread from the counter. "I made some chicken soup yesterday, from scratch. I even raised the chicken myself."

Emily was lost in thought, not sure she could sit here and make small talk when all she wanted was to grab Andi and kiss her. *What am I supposed to do with all these feelings?*

"Emily?"

Emily stood and took a step toward Andi. "What would you say if I offered you a kidney?"

"I would say thanks, I'm always looking for new body parts to add to my collection. Why? Do you have extra kidneys you're trying to get rid of?"

Yes, she knew without a doubt she had feelings for Andi. Strong feelings. "I like that answer." Emily swallowed hard, her eyes never leaving Andi's. "And...and...I have feelings for you." She wrung her hands together. "What I mean is, I have feelings beyond friendship for you." She couldn't help the few tears that escaped her eyes. She stood there feeling foolish and scared, her entire body hot with fear as she waited for a response from Andi.

But Andi didn't respond, and Emily was sure she'd made a huge mistake and was going to lose Andi forever. "Please say something," Emily said. *Damn it!* She'd blown it. She should have kept her big mouth closed. *Damn it! Damn it! Damn it!*

"Are you sure?"

Now would be a good time to take it back. To tell Andi that she was only kidding, that it was all a big joke. But she knew she couldn't do that. "I have never been more sure of anything in my entire life."

After what seemed like an eternity, Andi spoke. "I want you to be sure, Emily. All of this is very new to you. I want you to be sure. I couldn't take it if I confessed that I have feelings for you too, and you weren't sure."

"What did you say?" Emily couldn't keep the smile off her face.

"I said, I feel the same." Andi stood stock still. "So what should we do about this?"

"Any chance you could put down that bread and come over here and kiss me?"

Andi dropped the bread on the floor and closed the distance between them. She ran her hand over Emily's cheek and over her lips, leaving a hot trail across Emily's skin. Emily closed her eyes as Andi's lips touched her own. The kiss was soft and gentle and quick. Too quick. Andi pulled back. Emily opened her eyes to discover Andi looking at her.

"Are you sure?" Andi asked again.

"What does this tell you?" Emily slipped her hand behind Andi's head and pulled Andi's mouth to hers. Emily's tongue slipped into Andi's mouth and she could feel her tongue come forward to meet it. Andi's arms snaked around her, pulling her in tighter. She could feel the firm flesh of Andi's breasts press against hers. Every fiber of her body was alive with excitement. Andi was stirring feelings in her that she didn't even know existed. The kiss seemed endless and at the same time seemed but a moment.

"What about playing the field?" Andi asked.

"I played the field. Luckily it was a very small field."

Andi held her tight, yet with so much tenderness. "Oh yeah?"

"Yeah, actually it was more like a vacant lot."

"Well, I am very glad you're done playing in it." She kissed Emily's nose, her cheek, her temples, her lips.

"I'm done playing there, but I've just started playing here. Wanna play?" She kissed Andi again.

"Are you saying you're only playing?"

"Playing, kissing, loving, committing, I want all of it. I want all of you. What do you think?" Her lips went to Andi's neck and her hands went to Andi's hair. Emily ran her tongue from Andi's collarbone to her chin. Her tongue continued over the chin and directly to Andi's mouth and she kissed her deeply. She pulled back enough to ask, "Well? What do you think? Can we have it all?"

Andi's hands moved down Emily's back and cupped her rear. She pulled her in closer and Emily let out a small gasp. "You can have anything you want. Anything."

"Then I want you." She pulled Andi's mouth to hers and kissed her deeply. Her tongue danced around Andi's mouth, staking its claim. It was several minutes before Emily came up for air. "Right now." She made full contact with Andi's mouth again, this time with a new urgency. Emily's hands moved along Andi's back and down to the edge of her shirt. She slipped her hands underneath it. The contact with Andi's flesh made her fingers tingle. She couldn't believe how silky soft Andi's skin felt. One hand traveled up Andi's back in an attempt to undo her bra. The other couldn't wait that long and traveled around the front, squeezing Andi's breast through the material. Even through the cloth, Emily could feel Andi's nipple standing at attention.

Andi pulled back, putting some distance between them, breaking the kiss. Emily felt the loss of Andi's mouth and let out a small whimper of disappointment. She attempted to capture Andi's mouth again, but Andi put a hand up, stopping her.

Emily opened her eyes. Her heart threatened to beat right out of her chest. Her heavy breathing was matched breath for breath by Andi's. She tried to ask the question with her eyes because she wasn't sure she had the ability to speak. When Andi didn't answer, Emily suspected she might be having trouble as well.

When at last her heart and breath slowed enough, Emily spoke, her voice breaking. "Why..." She cleared her throat and started again. "Why did you stop?"

"Because I don't want to rush this."

"Don't you want me?" Emily tried to keep the fear from her voice.

"Yes, I want you. But I want this to be right for you. I want us to be girlfriends for a little while before we become lovers." Her brown eyes darkened and Emily could see the want in them.

"So what do you figure? Like an hour?" Emily attempted once again to resume the kiss.

"I was thinking more like a week," Andi said.

Emily pulled back. "A week. I can't wait a week. I was thinking an hour was too long."

"We can handle a week." She smiled.

Emily lips longed for more contact. She didn't feel much like smiling. "I'm not sure I can handle ten minutes."

Andi kissed her nose. "Yes, you can." She gingerly pulled Emily's hand away from her breast and out of her shirt.

Emily's fingers trailed over Andi's skin as she allowed her hand to be moved. She could see in Andi's eyes that she was as affected by the contact as Emily was. She hoped Andi would rethink her decision.

"One week," Andi said again, this time with obvious difficulty. She gave Emily a slow, tender kiss before releasing her hand and stepping away.

Andi picked up the loaf of bread from the floor, walked to the counter, and opened the Tupperware container of soup.

Emily didn't move. *One week? One week.*

"Sit down and I'll make us lunch."

Emily sat in the closest chair. She willed her blood away from her throbbing groin and back into her extremities and head. *A week. Okay, I can wait a week.* That was only seven days, right? Or maybe only five days, maybe it would be next Friday, like the end of this week. Should she ask? No, she'd sound like an idiot. Pretty sure she'd made a big enough idiot of herself already today.

"So, when you say a week, do you mean a full seven days or maybe just until Friday?" Emily scrunched up her face. *Nice!* She couldn't help herself.

Andi burst out laughing and Emily couldn't help but smile. "We'll see," Andi said. She crouched down in front of Emily and took both of Emily's hands in hers. "I'm so glad you told me."

"Me too. But right now, I'm trying not to slide off this chair."

Andi smiled wide, dimples in tow.

Okay, I can wait a week for this woman. I can wait the rest of my life for her. She is so worth it. "By the way, do you want to have dinner with me on Friday?" It was all Emily could do not to push Andi over backward and leap on top of her.

"I would love to have dinner with you on Friday." Andi stood up. "How about we get through lunch today first?" She kissed the top of Emily's head and went back to the business of making lunch.

Friday couldn't come soon enough.

CHAPTER TWENTY-ONE

Emily found herself constantly watching the clock. She seemed to be counting the minutes instead of the days until Friday. "It's all about light and shadow," Emily said to her Monday morning class. "Where is your light source coming from? What colors are your cast shadows? And no, shadows aren't black or gr—"

She was interrupted by a knock on the door. Emily opened it and came face-to-face with a large bouquet of flowers. Red roses, burgundy carnations, pink alstroemeria, and baby's breath made their way into the room carried by Mrs. Bowman, the office secretary. She set them down on Emily's desk.

"These are for you," she said. She lowered her voice and put the side of her hand near her mouth. "The card says, 'Thinking of you' and it's signed with the letter 'A.'" She winked at Emily, and Emily thought for a moment she might even smile. "A very lucky guy, this 'A' fellow," Mrs. Bowman said under her breath as she left the room, closing the door behind.

The room erupted into laughter.

"Okay, everybody settle down." Emily told them. But she couldn't contain her smile. She slipped the card into her pocket. *Thinking of you. Right back atcha, A.*

❖

Emily was hoping to catch Andi alone in her classroom before she left for lunch today. Alone time with her while working was rare, and they both agreed that a public high school wasn't the place to be showing affection. So there would be no touching or sneaked kisses. Emily knew it would take a lot of effort on her part to keep from looking longingly at Andi when others were around. She decided to avoid looking at her at all unless they were alone. Easier said than done.

Emily took the short trek to Andi's room and stuck her head in the open door. "Got a minute?" Emily asked, as casually as she could.

Andi looked up from the papers she was grading and smiled. "I do indeed, Miss Sanders. Come in, and feel free to close the door behind you."

Emily did as she was told and strolled over to Andi's desk. "Hi."

"Hi yourself."

"Thank you for the flowers. They're beautiful."

"Beautiful flowers for a beautiful lady."

"Mindy wanted me to ask you if you would come over tonight to help her pass out candy for Halloween."

"Mindy wants me there, huh?"

"Yes, Mindy. Oh, I'll probably talk to you too, while you're there. It wouldn't kill me, I guess." Emily tried to suppress a grin, but it broke free anyway.

"Yes, in that case, I would love to—for Mindy. I didn't get too many kids at my house last year and I ended up eating most of the candy myself. This will save me from the same fate. What time should I come over?"

"Why don't you come after work and have supper with us," Emily said.

"That sounds great. All right if I run home and change first?"

"I kind of like you just the way you are. But if you insist, I guess that would be fine. Are you going to the teachers' lounge for lunch today?"

"I have to catch up on grading." Andi held up a stack of papers. "But I am going to try to get there if I can. If I don't see you there, then I'll see you after work."

"Okay, don't work too hard." Emily headed in the direction of the teachers' lounge, looking forward to seeing Andi later.

❖

"Mindy, would you get the door, please," Emily yelled from the kitchen. "It's probably Andi."

She heard Mindy get up from the couch and go to the door. Mindy let out a sound that was half scream and half laugh. Emily came out of the kitchen wiping her hands on a dish towel. Standing in her doorway was a giant monkey. Shaggy black fur, big ears, and a red polka dot bow tie—yep, it was a monkey all right. The creature attempted to give Mindy a banana. She shook her head, put her hands over her mouth, and giggled.

The monkey offered the banana to Emily. She hesitated a moment before accepting the gift. "Why, thank you, Mr. Monkey," she said. "Or is it Miss Monkey?"

The monkey nodded.

Mindy broke out into another round of giggles.

"Would you like to come in?" Emily asked the monkey.

Another nod.

Emily took the monkey's hand and led it into the house. *I sure hope this is Andi. It might not be a good idea to let just any old monkey off the street into the house.* "Andi?" Emily asked.

The monkey stared at her for several seconds before it bobbed its head in affirmation.

When they got to the living room Emily said, "Would you care to take your head off?"

Andi pulled the head of the costume off, sending Mindy into another laughing fit. "What kind of a question is that to ask a guest? Would you care to take your head off? And you should be much more careful about who you let into your house."

"Apparently so," Emily teased. "Where did you get this thing?"

"What do you mean, where did I get it? I had it hanging in my closet. Doesn't everyone have a monkey suit hanging in their closet?"

"I don't," Mindy said between giggles.

"Well, you should," Andi told her. "How would you like to put this on after supper so you can answer the door and pass out candy to all the little kids? They'll think you're a real monkey." Andi looked at Emily. "That is, if it's all right with your sister here."

Mindy jumped up and down. "Oh p-p-please, can I be like a real monkey and p-p-pass out candy, Emily? P-please."

"Sure you can, honey."

"Can I do it now, p-pleeease?"

"How about I take it off now and you can put it on right after we eat. I promise. That way you don't have to worry about trying to eat in it. All right?" Andi turned around. "Here, Mindy, can you unzip the back for me and I'll take it off."

Emily interrupted. "I'm going to go finish making supper while the two of you are doing that."

"Do you need any help?" Andi asked.

"Nope, but you can help Mindy get the candy ready for tonight. Mindy knows where everything is." Emily went back into the kitchen.

Thirty minutes later they were sitting down to a dinner of rib eye steak, mashed potatoes, salad, and peas.

"Andi, p-p-please pass the p-peas?" Mindy asked.

"Sure, here you go." Andi passed her the bowl.

"Hey, how come you eat peas and they're mushy but you won't eat mushy baked beans?" Emily asked her sister.

"'Cause peas are green mushy. I like green mushy better." Mindy pushed her glasses farther up on her nose.

"Well then, I guess that explains it."

"Andi how come you are s-smiling so much today?" Mindy asked. "Isn't your face getting tired smiling so big?"

Andi glanced at Emily. "I guess I am just really, really happy today. Haven't you ever had a day when you were really, really happy Mindy?"

"I am really, really happy every d-d-day," Mindy answered. "But my face can't smile that much." She grinned. "See, this it as much as I can smile. But you are smiling really big."

"I'll try to keep it under control," Andi said. But her smile didn't lessen.

"Andi, could you please help me with something in my room?" Emily said nonchalantly to Andi, after they'd cleared the table. "Mindy, would you mind putting the rest of the dishes in the dishwasher and then go wait for us in the living room? We'll be back in a few minutes."

Andi threw a look at Emily that said *Are you sure we should do this?* Emily nodded her head, took Andi's hand, and led her to the bedroom.

"I am so sorry," Emily said.

"What are you sorry for?"

"Because I couldn't wait another moment before doing this." Her mouth crashed into Andi's, her kiss strong and demanding. Emily's tongue caressed the inside of Andi's mouth, searching for her tongue. When their tongues collided, it sent shivers down Emily's spine. The stars and sun were created with that kiss, and Emily was pulled into a black hole. She fully intended to pull Andi in with her.

Emily ran her tongue up to the roof of Andi's mouth and Andi took that opportunity to slip her tongue under Emily's. She slowly massaged the underside of Emily's tongue. Emily moaned deep in her throat. No one had ever kissed her like that before. She had trouble remaining on her feet. *I need to sit down before I collapse.* She started the downward motion onto the bed, but strong arms held her up.

❖

Andi knew that if they landed on the bed, she wouldn't be able to control herself. "Oh, no. No, you don't. I checked the calendar before I came over here, and today is only Monday." Andi's voice came out in gasps.

"I wasn't trying to cheat. I'm having trouble standing," Emily said, in a voice so husky that it took away the little bit of breath that remained in Andi's body.

"Uh-huh."

"I'm telling you the truth. I had no intention of seducing you, at least not with my sister only a room away. It's the truth," Emily said again. "I've never lied to you. Oh, except about my feet being sensitive. I made you stop touching them because it was starting to turn me on and—oh, never mind."

"Oh no, you are going to finish that sentence and then we're going to get back out there with Mindy before she comes looking for us." *Or before I totally lose what little self-control I have left.*

"Yes. We should do that," Emily said. She pulled Andi's mouth back to hers. It was another fifteen minutes before Emily and Andi emerged from the bedroom.

Mindy sat on the couch with the monkey suit on her lap. "What t-t-took you guys so long? I been waiting forever. I want be a monkey."

"Then let's get it on you. Bring it here," Andi told her. "You are going to have to take off your shoes. You can put them back on after the costume is on you if you want."

"No, monkeys do not wear shoes." Mindy giggled.

"All right then, no shoes." Andi helped Mindy step into the outfit and pull it up. She zipped up the back.

"Now the head. Now the head," Mindy chanted.

"Maybe we should put the head on you when the kids start coming for trick-or-treating," Emily told her.

"No, now. Can I have it on now, p-p-please?"

"Okay, but you need to take it off if you get too hot," Emily said.

"I will. I will." Mindy jumped up and down. Andi helped her pull the monkey head on, being careful of Mindy's glasses.

"Can you see in there?" Andi asked.

A muffled sound came from the head.

"I can't hear you. Nod if you can see."

The monkey head nodded.

"Can you breathe in there?"

Another nod.

Andi looked at Emily, who was trying to suppress a laugh. "I'm going to help you sit on the chair and you can wait for the doorbell to ring. Want me to turn the television on so you can watch it while you wait?" More nodding.

Andi led Mindy to the recliner and eased her down. She turned the television on and found a rerun of *Friends* for her to watch. Emily sat down on the couch and Andi sat down next to her to wait for the first of the trick-or-treaters to arrive. Andi slid her hand discreetly into Emily's. She thought Emily would be the one having trouble waiting until Friday, but she was finding it a struggle. *Four more days*, she told herself. *Four more days until I make this beautiful woman mine.*

CHAPTER TWENTY-TWO

H ow much time do we have left?" Emily said to Andi.
Andi looked at her watch. "About fifteen minutes."

"Then you need to hurry up and put it in. We don't have all day, and you keep missing the hole. I thought you said you were an expert at this." She shook her head in mock frustration.

"I've been doing this longer than you've been alive," Andi teased.

"Then that means you would have done it for the first time when you were like two. Am I supposed to believe that?"

"It's the truth. I was advanced for my age."

"Then why are you having trouble doing it now?"

"You're making me nervous. You're too close, and I can't move right. You need to move back a little."

Emily took two steps back. Andi took a practice swing and then hit the golf ball a little too hard. It rolled toward the hole and then about a foot past it. She looked up at Emily, who only shook her head. Andi walked to the ball and took another swing, using much less force this time. It rolled slowly to the cup and stopped two inches short of it.

Emily growled.

Andi took one last hit and the ball went right into the clown's nose. "That was a bogey, right?" she asked. Emily was keeping score.

"Um, let me think. Par on that hole was three. So four would have made it a bogey, and let me count here…oh yeah, you took eighteen swings. So, in fact, that wasn't a bogey. Now let's get going so I'm not late picking up Mindy."

❖

Dried leaves scampered across the driveway as Emily waited for the garage door to go up. Mindy had talked nonstop the whole ride home. She'd spent a couple of hours at Daisy's house after her day at Mirique Works, and she was excited to tell Emily and Andi all about it. They listened patiently and asked questions at all the right places. Emily pulled into the garage. The three women filed out of the car and into the house.

"Okay, Mindy, time to get dinner started. You can finish your story when we sit down to eat."

Mindy skipped off to her room while Andi and Emily walked to the kitchen.

"Tell me what to do, honey," Andi said.

"I wasn't aware that you would need instruction." Emily winked.

"I meant with supper, lady. You need to get your mind on cooking, 'cause I'm hungry." Andi's dimples took over her smile.

Emily tossed a box of macaroni and cheese to her. "Here ya go. Get cooking." She handed her a pan from the bottom cabinet.

Emily's expression turned serious. "I was thinking I should tell Mindy about us. I'm not sure how much of it she would understand, but I think it would be easier if Mindy knew. As it is now, I can't even hold your hand in front of her. I mean, what if at some point I want to throw you on the kitchen floor and make out with you?"

"Well, I don't think you would be doing that with your sister in the house, even if she did know."

"Why not? It's not as if she isn't capable of stepping over us if she wants to get a glass of milk."

"You are so bad." Dimples again.

"Yeah, but you love it."

"I do. Now get out of my way. I have macaroni and cheese to make." Andi shook the box for emphasis.

Mindy continued her story about her visit to Daisy's house throughout the meal. When they finished eating, Emily sent Mindy into the living room to find a movie on Netflix while she and Andi cleaned up the dishes.

Emily cornered Andi in the small pantry off the kitchen and planted several long wet kisses on her, which were readily returned. The sound of Mindy's voice calling them pulled them out of their embrace, and they trudged into the living room.

Mindy looked up from the TV as the two women came into the room. "Geez, what t-t-took you so long? I thought I might have to call the police or something."

Emily and Andi looked at each other and burst out laughing.

"What's so funny?" Mindy asked.

"Nothing. Nothing at all." Emily giggled. "Want to restart this movie so we can all see the beginning? And hop over to the chair so Andi and I can sit on the couch, please."

Mindy changed seats, pulled the lever on the side of the chair to bring up the footrest, and restarted the movie.

Andi and Emily sat close together on the couch. Emily reached over and turned off the lamp so the only light in the room was coming from the television. She pulled her feet up under her.

"I almost forgot. Would you like a glass of wine?" she whispered to Andi.

"No, thanks. I have everything I need right here." She discreetly took Emily's hand.

Emily loved the feeling of Andi's hand in hers. The softness and warmth astounded her. When Andi began to slowly run her fingertips up and down her arm, Emily's breath caught in her throat.

"Too much?" Andi whispered, obviously amused.

"You're driving me crazy. I may have to leave the room

before I attack you," Emily whispered directly into Andi's ear, and then licked the edge of it.

"Oh, so not fair."

Emily smiled in the dark. She squeezed Andi's hand and did her best to turn her attention to the movie. She drifted off to sleep somewhere around the middle. Her head rested on Andi's shoulder and the credits rolled on the TV screen when she woke up.

"I going to bed now. Good night, Andi. Good night, sleepyhead Emily," Mindy said.

"Good night, Mindy. Sweet dreams," Andi answered.

"Night, sweetie," Emily said.

"I would be happy to spend the night right here with you sleeping on my shoulder. But, I don't think you would be too comfortable in the morning if you slept with your neck at that angle."

"Were we sleeping together?" Emily said, still groggy from sleep. She smiled up at Andi.

"I am afraid you were sleeping by yourself." Andi kissed Emily's nose. "Since Mindy's gone to bed, I'm going to get going so you can get some rest."

"Rest, yes, I need all the rest I can get because I don't plan on sleeping at all this weekend." Emily sat upright, allowing Andi to extract herself. "Oh, and you might want to rest too, because I don't plan on you sleeping much either." She gave Andi a sly smile.

"You are so bad," Andi said. "Now, walk me to the door." She pulled Emily up, draped one arm around her, and walked side by side with her.

Andi gave Emily a quick kiss on the lips. "Gotta go." She turned and was gone before Emily had a chance to respond. Emily closed the door and leaned against it.

"Two more days," she said out loud. Two more days until Friday.

She locked the door, turned the lights off, and got ready for bed. Slipping under the covers, she opened the drawer of her nightstand and pulled out a book. She opened it to the bookmark and continued reading. She was almost done with this one, *How to Make Love to a Woman, the Lesbian Guide*, and would more than likely reread the two books she had already finished. She was going to be ready when Friday arrived...

CHAPTER TWENTY-THREE

Emily woke an hour before her alarm clock rang. It was Friday. Too excited and restless to sleep any longer, she sat up and stretched, surprised she'd slept at all. Her mind kept moving forward in time to the evening, Andi seated across from her at a nice restaurant, smiling and laughing. Fast-forward the scene to Andi kissing Emily and removing her clothing as they lay on Andi's bed.

Time for a cold shower.

She needed to cool down this porno flick running in her head. She let the cold water run over her for a few minutes before turning it to warm. She shampooed her hair and used the suds from the shampoo to wash her body, imagining they were Andi's hands instead of her own. She pushed the thought away. *I am going to spend the day in a pool of my own juices if I don't control my thoughts.* She was a grown-up, for God's sake, not a teenager with raging hormones. She could control her thoughts. She could. Oh, God, how was she going to get through the day when she couldn't control her thoughts?

❖

Emily pointed the car in the direction of the Waterloo Outlet Mall, halfway between Syracuse and Rochester, with Mindy in the passenger seat. The drive took forty-five minutes. Dad was already there waiting when they arrived.

"Dad, you look great," Emily kissed him on the cheek. "How are you doing?"

A clean shirt was neatly tucked into his dark blue pants. His coat looked new and Emily could tell that he had shaved that morning. His recent haircut made him look younger, and his smile was genuine.

"Doing good. I'm still missing your mom like crazy, but I figured I needed to start living my own life again."

Emily was starting to see her old dad emerge again. It was a great sight.

Mindy went around the car and set her suitcase down. She gave her father a tight hug. "Hi, Daddy. I missed you so much."

"I missed you too, kiddo. We're gonna have a great weekend. Ever played bingo?"

Mindy shook her head.

"That's okay. I'll show you how. I've been going every Saturday night. I think you'll like it." He put her suitcase in the trunk of his car.

"I need to get going, Dad. I have some stuff I need to take care of."

"We'll see you on Sunday. Drive safe." He gave her a hug. Emily watched them get into his car before backing out.

The traffic was light heading east on the Thruway, and Emily made good time. She made two stops before heading to her house to change. At the first, Vinnie's Wine and Liquor Store, she bought a bottle of Kendall-Jackson Grand Reserve Chardonnay, 2005. It was a very good year, the salesman told her. At the Pretty Petals Floral Shop, she headed directly to the roses. Emily knew that the different colors had different meanings, and she knew the common ones. Red for love. Yellow for friendship. But she was unsure of the other colors. Emily wanted the flowers to have an underlying meaning and not just play the role of being pretty.

"The white roses represent innocence and purity," the middle-aged saleswoman with stylish glasses explained.

I don't want that color, then.

"And are traditionally associated with new beginnings," the woman continued.

Oh, actually that's good. New beginnings. I like that. "How about the orange roses?" Emily asked.

"Desire and enthusiasm. That color often symbolizes passion and excitement and can be an expression of burning romance. And we also have the lavender roses here. These're my favorite. They're a symbol of enchantment. The lavender rose is also traditionally used to express feelings of love at first sight." Hmm, if it was love at first sight, it only took her two and a half months to figure it out. But she liked the enchantment part. She was definitely enchanted. "I'll take a dozen of each." Emily pictured herself trying to juggle a bottle of wine and five dozen roses. "Umm, better make that four red roses and two of each of the other colors." That would make an even dozen. *Andi would be proud of my quick math skills.*

❖

"How beautiful." Andi took the flowers Emily held out to her. "And you look nice too," she said, with a smile. "I take that back. You look stunning," Andi said, with total sincerity this time. Emily was glad she had taken extra time to pick out her clothes for the evening. She settled on a long-sleeved deep pink chambray shirt with a slight ruffle in the front, a fitted black blazer, and black dress slacks. Her earrings were Black Hills Gold dangle earrings in a stylishly longer length and a matching diamond accent pendant.

Andi's outfit was equally stunning in its casual elegance. Her tan button-down shirt made her brown eyes appear even darker. Skin peeked out at the top where several buttons were left undone. Her dark brown pinstriped pants had a small pleat in the front, and a thin matching brown belt circled her waist. Brown dress shoes replaced the sneakers that normally graced her feet. She kissed Emily on the cheek and gave her a quick hug. "Come in here," Andi purred. She took the bottle of wine from Emily and set it and the flowers on the hall table. She closed the door behind them and looked at Emily again. "Come here," she repeated, staring directly into Emily's eyes, her arms opened wide.

Emily closed the gap between them in an instant. Andi wrapped her arms around Emily and kissed her full on the mouth, pausing only a moment before letting her tongue enter Emily's mouth. Emily melted into the kiss. Everything in her began to throb. She was ready to forget about dinner and drag Andi off to bed now. The kiss went on for several long moments.

Finally, Andi let go of Emily. "That should keep us for a little while," she said. "But if I don't stop now, we won't make it out to dinner."

"We don't need to go to dinner. I'm not very hungry anyway." Emily struggled to catch her breath.

"Yes, we do. We're going out to a nice restaurant and on a wonderful date. I'll put these beautiful flowers in a vase and this wine in the fridge, and we can get going."

❖

The waiter set a plate of grilled flank steak salad in front of Emily and angel hair pasta primavera in front of Andi, asked if they needed anything else, then took his leave.

"So, how come you left so quickly on Wednesday night? You didn't even hug me." Emily asked the question that had been in the back of her mind since that evening.

"Truth be told, I didn't trust myself. I wanted so badly to hold you and kiss you and"—Andi lowered her voice—"make love to you. But I didn't want our first time to be…well, I didn't want to have to try to be quiet because someone else was in the next room. If you're a screamer, I want you to be able to scream," Andi said, with a sly grin and a slight blush.

"I have never screamed in my life," Emily informed her. She could feel her own blush creeping up her neck.

"Maybe you haven't ever been with the right person before."

"Considering I've never been with you, I would say I definitely have never been with the right person before. I know I have never felt for anyone what I feel for you." She fought the urge to lean across the table and kiss Andi. She settled for running a finger over the back of her hand. She could see the effect that small gesture had on Andi. "What do you say we pay the bill and get out of here?" Emily said, her voice throaty and low.

"What do you say we eat first?" Andi twirled her fork in her angel hair pasta and offered it across the table to Emily. Emily took a bite and dabbed at the corner of her mouth with a napkin.

"You really are beautiful, Emily."

Emily smiled. She wanted to look beautiful for Andi. "Thank you. I feel the same way about you. In fact, I'm crazy about you. Did I happen to mention that?"

"Yes, I think you've mentioned that a time or two."

"Remind me to tell you more often."

Andi smiled. Emily loved that smile. She picked at her food, enjoying it, the company and the thoughts of what was to come.

CHAPTER TWENTY-FOUR

Emily pulled her car into Andi's driveway.

"Would you like to come in for a drink?" Andi asked her. A smile tugged at the corners of her mouth.

Emily had trouble pulling her eyes away from that sexy mouth. "I believe I would. Thank you for asking. Let me get the door for you."

Andi sat patiently with a grin on her face as Emily walked around the car and opened the door. She offered her hand to Andi, who took it and eased out of the passenger side. They walked hand in hand to the door.

Once inside Andi poured two glasses of wine, took Emily's hand, and led her into the living room. After kicking off her shoes, Andi sat on the couch with one leg tucked under her and pulled Emily down beside her. Without a word, Andi took Emily's wine and set it next to hers on the side table. She took both of Emily's hands in hers and looked into her eyes. "Are you sure about this? Last chance to get out of it."

"Not on your life. I'm sure. Very sure. I want to be with you. I want to be with you in every way."

"Then I have to tell you that I can't wait another second. It's your choice if you would like to join me in my bedroom or if you would like me to attack you right—" The words were cut off by Emily's kiss.

Emily's mouth left Andi's long enough for her to move it to Andi's ear. Her tongue flicked the edge of it as she said, "Bedroom."

Andi rose, pulled Emily up with her and pulled her in close. Their bodies fit together as if they'd been formed for each other. Andi's hand traveled up over Emily's back and into her hair as their lips found each other again.

Emily pulled the tail end of Andi's shirt out of her pants and slid her hand where the shirttail had been. Her hands slid over silky underwear and she pulled Andi even closer.

Andi made a weak attempt to walk Emily backward toward her room but failed. "We aren't going to make it to the bedroom this way."

Without another word, Emily turned, grabbed the waistband of Andi's slacks, and pulled her toward the bedroom. Once in the room, she turned again to Andi and kissed her deeply. Her hands found the buttons on Andi's shirt. She undid each one and pushed the shirt off her shoulders. It fell to the floor. The bra quickly followed. Emily slid her hands down Andi's bare arms, feeling the softness of skin and the tightness of the muscles beneath. Emily pulled out of the kiss and looked into Andi's eyes as her hand found her breasts. Her brown eyes darkened as her body reacted to Emily's touch.

She couldn't believe how wonderful it felt to touch Andi. Couldn't believe her own boldness. She didn't seem to be able to control herself. She felt like she had been waiting for this moment her whole life. She had.

Emily's lips brushed once again over Andi's lips before traveling down her chin to her neck and chest. Andi's breath caught in her throat when the kisses reached her breast and she took a nipple into her mouth. Her lips and tongue went to work bathing it while her fingers massaged Andi's other breast. Nipples hardened beneath her touch.

Emily's arousal soaked her underwear. She found the zipper

on Andi's pants and quickly undid them, sliding the slacks down silky-smooth legs.

Andi pulled Emily's face back up to hers and kissed her deeply as she stepped out of the pile of clothes and kicked them away. Andi deftly removed Emily's shirt and bra and let them fall to the floor. In one swift move, pants and underwear joined the rest of the discarded clothes.

A hot chill ran through Emily as Andi's hands slid up her sides to her breasts. The nipples stood tall to meet the palms of Andi's hands while her fingers caressed the sides of Emily's flesh.

Only Andi's underwear stood between the total melding of their two bodies. Without conscious thought, Emily remedied the situation, and the offending piece of clothing landed on the floor.

Andi's fingers worked their way up Emily's neck until they reached her earlobes. She gently removed Emily's earrings and set them safely on the nightstand. "I want you totally naked."

The sound of Andi's voice only managed to cause another surge of wetness.

Andi's strong arms circled Emily as she lowered her to the bed and settled on top of her. Andi's thigh came down between Emily's legs, and Emily let out a moan at the pressure. The moan was pushed back into her mouth by Andi's tongue as she kissed her hard. Andi's hands once again explored Emily's body.

With each kiss and caress, Emily felt as if Andi were breathing life into her very soul. She had never before experienced this depth of feeling. The physical sensations were matched by the emotional connection she felt for Andi. Emily sucked in a lungful of air when Andi's thigh between her legs was replaced by Andi's hand.

"You are so wet."

"It's all for you." Emily breathing was rapid and her hips undulated against Andi's hand. Without warning, Andi slipped a finger inside her, quickly followed by another. Andi moved her fingers expertly through the slickness. Her fingers settled on the small spongy spot inside Emily and made small circular motions as her thumb rubbed between the moist folds of Emily's mound. Feelings overwhelmed Emily. Her hips matched the movements of Andi's hand, and it was only a matter of moments before her body exploded and spasms took over. Andi increased the speed of her fingers for several seconds before stilling them and letting Emily's body ride her hand.

"Oh God," Emily moaned. A small scream escaped from the back of her throat.

Andi waited until Emily's hips stopped moving before slipping her fingers out. She wrapped her arms around Emily and held her until her breathing slowed and returned to normal.

"I believe I heard a scream come out of that pretty little mouth of yours."

Emily could hear the smile in Andi's voice. "I can't believe what you do to me. I have never…never so fast…never so hard…I…well…I just never."

"Well said." Andi kissed the top of her head.

"I'm not sure I can do the same for you," Emily admitted. She certainly wanted to try, but her lack of experience worried her.

"You don't have to do anything you don't want to do." Andi pulled the tangle of blankets up over them both.

"I want to do everything to you. I've just never done it before, so I'm not sure what to do. How to do it." Emily looked up into Andi's eyes.

"Do what would feel good to *you*. I love being with you, so anything you do will be perfect."

"Will you help me?" Emily suddenly felt shy.

"I'll do anything you want me to do. Anything."

Emily gently pushed Andi onto her back. Her hand went immediately to Andi's breast. Her fingers began a slow caress while Emily's lips found Andi's mouth. Emily's tongue washed over Andi's lips before entering her mouth. Emily savored the kiss. "I thought I would try starting out like this," Emily said.

"What an excellent way to start." Andi smiled briefly as her breathing took on a ragged edge. "You're doing great so far."

Emily kneaded one breast while her mouth and tongue licked the nipple of the other.

"Oh, yeah, you're definitely getting the hang of this."

Emily lifted her face to Andi's. "I want to taste you. Is that all right?"

Andi nodded and pulled Emily into a deep kiss that left them both gasping for air.

Emily pulled the blankets off, turned, and lowered her face to Andi's center. She ran a tentative finger over Andi's already swollen flesh. She felt a surge in her own body as she felt Andi's wetness. Her own body reacted when she heard Andi suck in her breath as Emily tentatively allowed her tongue to find what it was seeking. The scent and taste of Andi was overwhelming. Emily's own arousal grew as she found the secret folds and crevices of Andi's body.

Her instincts took over, and Emily moved her mouth and tongue over and into Andi without hesitation. Andi's pleasure became her pleasure.

Andi's heels dug into the mattress as her hips rose to meet Emily's mouth. Her hands came down on the back of Emily's head and held her there as Andi's breath became more and more ragged and caught in her throat. Her release came in waves and crashed around her.

Emily moved up to hold Andi in her arms. She curled into her, molding her body to the heat of Andi's, as Andi slowly came down from the crest of the wave she was riding.

She lifted Emily's chin and planted a moist kiss on her mouth. "For someone who doesn't know what they're doing, you sure know what you're doing."

Emily liked the taste of Andi's arousal on her lips. "I cheated," Emily said with a sly grin.

"Should I ask?" Andi raised an eyebrow.

"I bought some books and read them cover to cover. Several times. But you made it easy for me."

"How so?" Andi still held her chin as she looked into Emily's eyes.

"I listened to your breathing and those other wondrous sounds coming out of you. I could tell what you liked."

"Well, I like you." Andi kissed her again.

They drifted off to a peaceful but short-lived sleep, wrapped up in each other's arms.

❖

"How come you didn't tell me how you felt before I told you?" Emily dragged the back of her fingernails across Andi's stomach and watched as the skin broke out in goose bumps.

"At the beginning, I thought you were straight, so I figured that letting you know would scare the hell out of you, and I didn't want to risk losing you as a friend." Andi paused. "Then when you told me that you were gay, I was about to tell you, but you told me that you met someone and, well, it didn't seem right to say anything."

"And after that? After it was over with Sarah?" Emily looked into Andi's eyes as the moonlight from the window danced over her face. "Why didn't you say anything then?"

"You said you wanted to play the field, and I thought I should let you. But I have been in enamored of you since the first moment I met you."

Emily smiled. "You are so full of shit."

"Okay, maybe not since the first moment, but I did think you had a really nice butt the first time I saw you, all bent over picking up papers." She kissed Emily on the nose. "It didn't take me long to fall for you. Not long at all."

Emily's tone turned serious. "What if I had met someone while I was playing the field?"

"Emily, I care about you and I want you to be happy. So, if that meant that you were happy with someone besides me, well then, I guess I would have been happy for you. But in all honesty, if that had happened, I think a piece of me would have died inside. I am so glad, so unbelievably glad, that you fell for me."

Tears flooded Emily's eyes. "I wish I'd realized sooner. I'm sorry I put you through that. I wish you were the first woman I ever kissed."

Andi kissed away the tears as they escaped down Emily's cheek. "Shh," she said. "It's okay that I wasn't your first kiss, baby. You needed to experience what you experienced."

"So, then I could come back to you whole and complete?" Emily couldn't help but smile through her tears as she remembered what Andi said about that Tom Cruise movie.

"Something like that. Besides, now you know for sure that I'm the best." A broad smile covered her face, bringing the dimples out with it.

"A little conceited, aren't we?"

Andi gave Emily's ribs a quick tickle. "Admit it! Admit that I'm the best." She leaned over and glided her tongue up Emily's chest, beginning right above her belly button and around each nipple. "Admit it," she said, bringing her face back up to Emily's.

"I admit it. The best."

Andi rolled Emily onto her back and climbed on top of her. She kissed Emily briefly on the lips before moving downward, leaving a trail of kisses in her wake until she reached the spot she was aiming for. Emily's hips rose to meet Andi's mouth and they both moaned as contact was made.

CHAPTER TWENTY-FIVE

Warm sunshine filtered through the open window, soaking the room in light. Andi awoke from a sound sleep to a soft nuzzling in her ear. She lay still for several seconds with her eyes still closed, enjoying the feeling. Her eye opened instantly when Emily laughed from across the room. Andi turned her head toward the nuzzling and came face-to-face with Butch.

"Hey, how did you get here?" Andi said to the cat.

"She was scratching on the bedroom door, so I let her in. I also refilled her food and water bowls." Emily held up a cup. "And I made you coffee. Guess I have to do everything around here." She had put on a gray T-shirt she must have found in Andi's drawer, but hadn't bothered to put any underwear on.

"You poor baby. You must be so tired from doing all that. Come here and let me do something for you for a change." Andi opened her arms to Emily.

Emily set the cup of coffee down on the nightstand and crawled into Andi's arms. Butch must have decided that the bed was too crowded. She jumped down and stomped out of the room as if she had been insulted.

"I guess we pissed her off," Emily said.

"She'll get over it. She always does—whenever I have a beautiful, naked woman in my bed."

Emily swatted at Andi. "Hey! How many beautiful women

have you had in this bed? Never mind. I don't want to know, and besides, I'm not naked."

Andi tugged at her shirt. "Let's see if we can't fix that." Andi pulled the shirt over Emily's head and threw it on the foot of the bed. "And truth be known, you are the only beautiful woman that I've had naked in this bed. The rest were kind of ugly." Andi got swatted again.

"Hey!"

"I'm kidding. You are the only woman I ever want in my bed, ever. How's that?" She kissed Emily softly on the lips.

The kiss deepened.

Andi's coffee got cold…

❖

"I'll make another pot," Andi said, pouring the almost full container of coffee down the drain. "Why don't you sit and I'll make us breakfast." She couldn't remember the last time she had been this happy.

"I think it would be lunch. It's after one. And I am famished. It's hard work loving you all night and half the morning."

"Are you complaining?" Andi asked.

Butch jumped up on the counter the same moment Andi pressed the start button on the coffeemaker. The machine made a loud noise as the whole beans started spinning and were ground to bits, falling into the filter to wait for the hot water to pass through them. The sound startled the cat and she jumped into the air, spun around, and half fell, half jumped off the counter and ran out of the kitchen.

They laughed. "I've made coffee in that thing the same way every day for the past year and a half. Every time it starts, that cat runs. I may have to change her name from Butch to Wuss." That brought about another round of laughter.

When the laughter died down, Emily said, "No. I'm not, by the way."

EMILY'S ART AND SOUL

Andi raised her eyebrows and tilted her head.

"Complaining. I'm not complaining. I could easily spend the rest of my life in bed making love with you. It would just be a short life because we would die of starvation before too long."

"I think we would die from lack of water before we starve to death," Andi said matter-of-factly.

"Does it have to be actual water or would any fluid do?" Emily asked. "'Cause I think we would have plenty of other fluids." A small snorting sound escaped her nose as she suppressed a giggle.

"I thought I had a dirty mind, but yours is worse." Andi threw a wadded paper towel at her.

Emily caught it in midair.

"You're good," Andi said.

"You make me want to be good. I want to be good for you, and yes, I am talking in the dirtiest way possible."

Andi shook her head. "What am I going to do with you?" She was sure she could think of a few things.

"How about I make you a list of everything you can do with me, while you make us lunch?" She grabbed a pad of paper and pen from the counter. She started to write. "How do you spell 'cunnilingus'?" Emily asked.

Andi stopped what she was doing and turned to Emily. "If you can't spell it, you don't get it." She turned back to the job at hand.

Emily stomped out of the room. "What are you doing?" Andi yelled to her.

Emily yelled back from the living room. "I'm looking for a dictionary. I don't want to risk spelling it wrong."

"Get your ass back in here, silly. I'm starting to miss you already."

Emily poked her head into the room. "So, you missed me, huh?" Emily seemed almost giddy.

"Yes, I admit it. I missed your beautiful face and your cute little butt when you were in the other room. That was the longest fifteen seconds of my life."

Andi finished making lunch and set a grilled cheese sandwich and a bowl of tomato soup in front of Emily with a theatrical flair. "For m'lady," she said, with a wave of her hand. "Eat fast. I can hear my bed calling us."

CHAPTER TWENTY-SIX

Sunday evening arrived way too quickly for Emily. She couldn't believe how wonderful spending the weekend with Andi had been. The sex had been amazing. Emily never realized how wonderful lovemaking could be.

"What time are you supposed to meet your dad and Mindy?" Andi asked.

"In about an hour." Emily sighed. She breathed in, smelling the scent that was Andi, and placed tiny kisses on her neck. She knew she had to get out of the bed and get moving.

"Are you sure you don't want me to go with you?"

"Thank you for offering, but yeah, I'm sure. I don't think I would make it there if you were with me. I would have to pull over at every rest stop and make love to you." Emily said between kisses.

"How many rest stops are there between here and Waterloo?"

Emily thought for a few seconds. "Two, I think."

"Let's see, that would be about forty-five minutes of actual driving and an hour at each rest stop. That would put you at the outlet mall way late."

"Only an hour at each rest stop?" Emily looked into Andi's smiling eyes, knowing that an hour wouldn't be enough time for everything she wanted to do to and with her.

"I was trying to keep you on schedule. Guess it can't be done." Andi squeezed Emily tighter. "I don't want to let you go."

"And I don't want to leave you, but I have to go pick up Mindy." She extracted herself from Andi's arms, missing them as soon as she slipped out of the bed. "Oh." A thought came to her. "Does this mean you have a new toaster oven coming to you?"

"It's not official till you get a cat." Andi grinned. She jumped up out of bed and wrapped her arms around Emily. "Dance with me before you go." Andi let go long enough to find a song on her iPhone. Soft music filled the air as she swayed with Emily. "How are you doing? Are you all right with everything that happened this weekend?" Andi asked her.

"I am doing more than all right. How come you're asking me that?"

"Because I know this is all new for you, and I want to make sure everything is—you are—all right?"

"I am so happy about this weekend and about you. The only thing that worries me…" She hesitated.

"Yes?" Andi said.

"I don't know how I'm going to be able to keep my hands off you in school tomorrow." Even the *thought* of seeing Andi and not being able to touch her was hard.

"I guess that is going to be a problem for both of us. Should I keep my distance?"

Emily didn't know if she was serious or not. She hoped she wasn't. "Don't you dare!"

"Okay, how about this? When I see you in the hall or the teacher's lounge or something, I'm going to ask you how your oil painting class is going and that will be code for *I want you so bad*. What do you think?"

"And how is that going to stop me from wanting to put my hands all over you?"

"Oh. Good point. I guess we'll have to meet behind the bleachers on the football field and make out."

An electric current ran through Emily at the thought. "You aren't helping here, and I hate to do this, but I have to get going."

Emily kissed Andi softly on the mouth. She grabbed her clothes from the end of the bed and slipped them on. She gave Andi a hug and another kiss. "I'll call you when I get home."

"I look forward to it."

Another soft lingering kiss and Emily reluctantly left, but she knew this was just the beginning of many long and blissful weekends with this wonderful woman.

CHAPTER TWENTY-SEVEN

The bell rang for the start of homeroom. All of the kids took their seats without a word from Emily, and Emily took attendance without the need to call names.

With the small amount of sleep she had gotten over the weekend, Emily should have been exhausted, but she felt exhilarated instead. It was as if Andi had touched her very soul this past weekend and breathed life into her. The mere thought of what they had done, the love they had made, sent a tingle down into the pit of her stomach before settling lower. She knew she had to keep her mind on teaching today. She didn't need her students seeing her staring off into space, her thoughts on Andi.

The bell rang again and most of the kids filed out of her classroom and into the hall. Emily concentrated on the sounds of laughter and locker doors opening and closing. Her first-period students trickled in.

"Good morning, everyone," Emily said. "Today we're going to watch a movie about Michelangelo and the Renaissance period. Can anyone tell me something about Michelangelo? Tony?" He'd been talking nonstop to his girlfriend since entering the room.

"Um, he painted during the Renaissance period?"

"Are you asking me or telling me?"

"Asking you?" Tony said.

Emily didn't respond and kept her gaze steady.

"Telling you?"

The class erupted with laughter.

"Can we narrow it down to one of those two choices?" She expected certain things from her students. One was paying attention and the other was confidence, both with their answers and with their art. "Try again."

"Michelangelo was a painter during the Renaissance period." He said it with certainty this time.

"Good. Much better. Now, who can tell me something about the Renaissance period? When did it start?" She looked around the room. "Jamie?"

"The fourteenth century."

"Very good," Emily said. "Jessica, name another artist who was painting during the Renaissance period."

"Was it Leonardo da Vinci?" She caught herself and said, "I mean, Leonardo da Vinci."

"Wow, you guys are good. Maybe we don't need to watch this movie and I'll give you a test instead."

Emily smiled when they groaned.

"Steven, would you mind pulling the screen down and pull the DVD projector to the middle of the room?"

Emily started the movie and shut off the overhead lights by the door. She closed the door partway and leaned against the wall next to it. She could see the movie from this vantage point and still keep an eye on the kids. She willed herself to pay attention to the movie. She'd seen it before but needed a refresher so she could ask questions at its conclusion.

Emily jumped when she heard someone whisper directly behind her. "How is your oil painting class going?" The words and Andi so close caused a rush of moisture.

Emily pretended that she didn't know what Andi was talking about. "This is my art history class. Oil painting is at the end of the day."

"Oh, I thought you had oil painting classes all day long. Sorry, my mistake." A couple of students looked over as the teachers talked quietly. Emily pointed at the screen and the students turned their attention back to the movie.

"You know I would have oil painting classes all day and night if I could. But hey, I have to make a living, so I teach things like art history." Emily looked at the clock. "How come you aren't teaching a class right now?"

"My kids are taking a mock SAT test in the cafeteria, so I have a free period. Did you want to meet me at lunch behind the bleachers on the football field?" She kept her voice so low that even Emily had to strain to hear it.

"You are going to make me crazy. I can't do this here." She *needed* Andi to stop much more than she *wanted* her to stop. At this rate she was going to have to go home and change her underwear between classes.

"You're right. I'm sorry. I was trying to get you to smile. Forgive me?"

"I want so bad to tell you all about my oil painting class, but I can't do it here. I can meet you at your house after work if you'd like."

"After work would be fine. We can go over those, um, test papers you wanted me to see. Will I see you at lunch, Miss Sanders?"

"I believe you will Miss Marino. Have a good day." She gently pushed Andi out the door.

❖

Andi spotted Emily right away seated at one of the tables in the teachers' lounge when she arrived, a cafeteria tray in one hand and a bottle of spring water in the other. The room filled up fast as other teachers filed in on their lunch breaks.

Andi set the tray down on the table, taking note of the various dishes and a chocolate chip cookie that fought for space on Emily's crowded tray. She settled in next to Emily, sitting as close to her as possible without actually touching her. It only took a few seconds for Emily to move her leg, pushing it firmly against Andi's. Andi's body reacted immediately to the contact, momentarily making it hard for her to think.

"A little hungry, are we?" Andi asked her when she had composed herself.

"A little. I'm eating a big lunch because I need my strength for later." Emily took a bite of pizza.

Andi wasn't sure where Emily was going with this, but considering they weren't alone Andi hoped it wasn't going in the direction her mind and body was.

"I'm playing tennis after work. I thought I would try a little carb-loading so I could keep my stamina up. What do you think? Think it will help?" Emily's voice held no hint of flirtation or double entendre.

Andi could play this game. "I very recently started playing tennis myself. I find I can play on an empty stomach as easily as a full one. It doesn't seem to matter."

"Tennis is a great game. Are you enjoying it?" Emily asked.

"Oh my God, yes. I love it. Great exercise. It gets my heart pumping and my juices flowing." Andi could see a slight blush rising in Emily's cheeks. She knew her words were having an effect. But she wasn't the only one it was affecting. *Oh geez. I'm getting my juices flowing right now. Better stop all this talk about tennis.*

"I used to play tennis." Ed Hinkle sat down across from them and joined in the conversation. "I had to give it up. Bad knees."

Andi avoided eye contact with Emily. She knew she wouldn't be able to suppress the laughter if she did.

"Wow, Ed, that's too bad. Do you miss it?" Andi asked.

"Sure do. I pump iron now to keep in shape, but I liked having a partner. I work out by myself. It just isn't the same."

Andi thought she was going to die. She realized she was holding her breath. She tried to let it out slowly without drawing any attention to herself.

"I hear ya," Emily said. "It is always better doing it with

a partner than by yourself." Without looking at her she asked, "What do you think, Andi?"

"Huh?" Andi pretended to be engrossed in her sandwich.

"Ed and I both think it is better doing it with a partner than doing it by yourself. I was wondering what your thoughts are."

My first thought is that I am going to kill you. I am going to end up choking on my chicken salad sandwich if you keep this up. She knew Emily was looking at her, waiting for her answer. Guess this was payback for her talking about *oil painting* earlier. She took another bite of her food, to give herself more time to collect herself. "Having a partner is good. Why don't you find a workout partner to pump iron with, Ed?"

Mike Tadd sat down next to Ed. "I'll pump with you," he said to Ed. "I've been doing it by myself for a couple of years now, but I would love to have a partner to do it with."

Andi knew Emily was having way too much fun with this to let it die.

Emily continued. "I think that's a great idea, Ed, you could do it with Mike."

"They said it's going to snow on the TV," Andi said in a feeble attempt to change the subject.

"It's going to snow only on the TV? Is it going to snow anywhere else?" Emily asked.

"I think I said that wrong." Andi smiled at her own mistake.

"I believe that is what you call a dangling participle," Emily told her.

Andi laughed. "I could have sworn you were an art teacher, not an English teacher."

"I minored in English."

"Well, then," Andi said. "Thank you for helping me see the error of my ways. I will never make that mistake again."

"I decided recently that I am so done with dangling participles. In fact, I am done with anything that dangles."

Andi didn't dare respond for fear she would burst out laughing.

"Let me know if you need help with anything else, Andi. Spelling. Grammar. Tennis. Anything. I'm always glad to lend a hand."

Andi did her best to push the image of Emily's hand touching her most intimate spots from her mind, but not before it caused a stir in her body.

"Kind of early for snow," Ed said, jumping back into the conversation. "But I guess anything is possible in Syracuse."

"I like to think of it more as *everything* is possible in Syracuse," Emily said, slipping in a sideways glance at Andi.

Andi smiled. "I like that," she said. "I really like that."

❖

Emily sat at her desk in the empty classroom. She had a few things left to grade before heading over to Andi's house. Her cell phone rang, pulling her attention away from the stack of paintings. She reached into her backpack to retrieve it.

"Hello?"

"What are you wearing?" the husky voice on the phone asked.

"I'm totally naked," Emily deadpanned.

Andi laughed. "Ooh, that's what I was hoping to hear."

"And I was hoping to get an obscene phone call today. So I guess we both made out pretty darn good."

"I wanted to let you know that Mindy is more than welcome to come with you when you come over today."

"That is so nice of you, but I think it might be embarrassing for you when I rip all of your clothes off right there in the hallway. Besides, Mindy has plans for tonight with a friend from the center. So you're stuck with just me."

"In that case, maybe I'll just answer the door naked to save you the trouble."

"Oh, it's no trouble, trust me. I am almost done here, so how about I come over in about an hour?"

"I'll see you then, baby. Bye."

"Bye, honey." Emily smiled. Just hearing Andi's voice made her wet. She couldn't wait to see her in person.

❖

"Damn. I thought you were going to be naked when I got here," Emily said.

"I was cooking, and I was afraid of burning something important."

Emily wrapped her arms around Andi. "Hi, baby. How was your day?"

"Well, my lunch was a little difficult to get through because I thought I was going to choke on something. But I managed to survive."

"I'm glad. You know I would have given you mouth-to-mouth if you choked, right?"

"I appreciate that, but I think that would have been the wrong rescue technique for choking."

"I know, but I'll use any excuse I can to put my mouth on yours."

"You don't need an excuse. You just lean toward me and…" Andi demonstrated. "Come on into the kitchen so I can finish cooking." Andi took Emily's hand to lead her, but Emily didn't follow.

"I have something in the car. Let me go get it and I'll meet you in there."

"Need any help?" Andi asked.

"No, I can handle it. I'll be right back." She went out to her car, grabbed the package she'd wrapped in silver foil, and headed back into the house. She handed it to Andi.

"What's this for?"

"It's for you." Emily smiled. "I hope you like it."

"I'm sure I'll love it. What is it?"

"How about you open it and find out." Emily held her breath

as Andi pulled off the pink ribbon and bow and wrapping paper. She felt like she had put a piece of herself in that box.

Andi lifted the lid off the box, pushed aside white tissue paper, and pulled out a drawing, framed in dark gray wood with an elegant white linen liner. She gingerly ran her fingers over the glass, admiring the figure of the nude female. "Is this the drawing I saw in your studio the first time I went to your house?"

Emily nodded.

"It's beautiful, Em. I love it. Thank you so much."

"I started this a long time ago, long before I met you. I think somewhere in the back of my mind I knew I was gay and this was my *dream girl*. So, I guess that would make it a portrait of you."

Andi set the drawing back down and gathered Emily in her arms. "I love it."

"Maybe dinner can wait?" Emily asked. She had an appetite, but it wasn't for food.

CHAPTER TWENTY-EIGHT

I think I'm going to tell my dad about me—about us—when I go there for Thanksgiving," Emily said. It had been almost three weeks since Andi had become her lover. She felt like she was lying to her father whenever she talked to him on the phone or dropped Mindy off for a visit. She'd felt that way when she met him in Waterloo two days ago so Mindy could spend her vacation with him.

Andi kissed Emily on the top of the head as they lay together in Andi's bed, covered only by a sheet. "I know that's not an easy thing to do. Would it help if I was there with you?"

"I love you for offering, but this is something I need to do myself." The very thought of it made her nervous. She wasn't sure how her father was going to react, and if it didn't go well, having Andi there would only make it worse.

"Do you know what you are going to say?"

"I've run it through my head a million times." She grinned at Andi. "No, not literally. But I have thought about it a lot, and to answer your question, no, I'm not sure. I don't know what he's going to say either. If my mother were still alive, I think she would be okay with it. But with my dad, it's anybody's guess. I hate that you and I aren't spending Thanksgiving together. I don't want to miss spending Christmas with you too."

"I know, baby, me too." Andi stroked Emily's arm, offering her no advice for the daunting task before her.

❖

Emily drummed her fingers on the steering wheel as she drove to Rochester. She played the scene out in her head over and over again. She wasn't sure if she could explain why it took her until the age of thirty-five to figure out she was gay when she wasn't sure she fully understood it herself. She wanted to at least have her opening line ready before she arrived at her dad's house.

Dad, I think I'm gay. No, no, I don't think I'm gay, I know I'm gay.

That one wouldn't work.

Dad, do you remember how I never dated much in high school? Turns out I'm a big ol' lezzy, a queer, a dyke.

No. Come on, she had to think of something.

I met someone, Dad, and you are going to like him. Because he's a she.

Nope, she didn't want him to think that Andi influenced her in any way. She needed to tell him that she figured out the gay part before she got involved with Andi. *Okay, think. How can I do this?*

Emily was still running the possibilities through her head when she pulled into the driveway. It was beginning to get dark, but Emily could see that the lawn was mowed and her mom's flower garden had been weeded. The broken shutter on the front of the house was repaired. It looked like Dad was indeed doing better. She hoped this didn't set him back.

Suddenly, Emily felt like she couldn't breathe. She sat in the car willing herself to go into the house. *I can't sit here all night. Okay, here I go.* Moments stretched while she listened to the ticking of the engine. *Well, I seem to be still sitting in the car.* She decided to at least open the car door.

Without another moment's thought, Emily did so, stepped

out, and somehow managed to walk to the house. She was about to knock when the door swung open and Mindy threw herself into Emily for a hug.

"I missed you oh so m-much." Mindy squeezed her. She took Emily's hand and led her into the house. The smell of tomato sauce and garlic filled the air. She followed her nose to the kitchen.

"There she is," her father said. "We ate earlier, but I thought you might be hungry when you got here. Sit, sit. Do you want cheese with this?" He placed a plate of spaghetti and meatballs on the table.

Emily sat down. She ran her hand over the top of the old table, the same table that she had grown up with. The worn wood was as familiar to her as her childhood. A childhood filled with love. Filled with joy. Filled with Mom. She wished her mother were here now. "No cheese. This is great."

Mindy sat down in the chair across from her. "I sure did m-miss you, Emily."

"You too." The nerves in her stomach were settling down as the warm smell from her food wafted up. They made small talk as Emily ate.

"That was really good. Thanks." *Now or never. Confession time.* The anxiety bubbled back up. *I need to get this over with before I make myself sick.* "Hey, Mindy, why don't you go get my suitcase from the car and put it in my room." She pulled her keys from her pants pocket. "Would you mind doing that for me? Put your coat on, because it's getting really cold out. And don't forget to lock the car when you're done." Emily waited until she was out of the room. She looked over at her father. His back was to her as he rinsed a dish in the sink.

"Dad," she started.

He turned to her. "I really enjoyed our visit this week. Mindy and I had a good time," he said, with a smile.

"Sit down, Dad. There's something I need to talk to you

about." Tears filled her eyes. She caught them with the edge of her napkin and tried to smile. *Oh crap, don't start crying yet. You won't be able to talk.*

Her father's expression turned grave, the smile gone in an instant. He sat down next to her and waited for her to start. When she hesitated, he asked, "Are you sick? Is something wrong?"

"I'm fine, Dad. Nothing's wrong." She paused. "At least, I don't think it's wrong, and I am hoping you feel the same."

"What is it, honey?"

Emily cleared her throat. "I'm gay, Dad." She watched him, trying to gauge his reaction. Several long moments passed without him speaking. His smile didn't return. He looked down.

"Dad, please say something."

He brought his eyes up to Emily. "Is this a joke? Because if it is, Emily, it's not a very funny one."

"It's no joke. I'm gay. It took me a long ti—"

"This is nothing I ever expected from you," her father interrupted. "You decide that you're gay and I'm supposed to just accept it? Well, I don't."

Emily jumped as his chair scraped the floor and he stood up.

"I can't deal with this. I am finally getting myself straightened out here and dealing with your mother's death and you drop this on me. This isn't right."

"Dad, I-I didn't choose this. I…" Emily didn't know what to say. She hadn't been sure how her father would react, but she hadn't expected this. Tears flowed. The silence that filled the air was deafening.

"Dad?" Emily said, when she couldn't stand it any longer.

"Emily, you were raised right. We went to church every Sunday. You weren't exposed to those kinds of people. How can you be gay? Never mind. I don't want to hear the answer. I can't talk to you about this." He stomped out of the room.

Stunned, Emily slumped forward in her chair crying. She wasn't sure what to do, but she knew that she couldn't stay here.

She couldn't spend the night in this house and go to her aunt's house in the morning. She had to get out. All of the air had been sucked out of her lungs and she felt like she couldn't breathe.

Her father sat in the living room, staring off at nothing when she walked past him. She went up the stairs as Mindy was coming down.

"What a matter, Emily?" Mindy looked confused.

"I'm not feeling too good, honey. Go on downstairs with Dad and I'll be down in a minute. Okay?"

"Okay."

Emily washed her face in the bathroom and blew her nose. She grabbed her suitcase from the bedroom and headed back downstairs. "I'm going to go home. Do you want me to take Mindy with me?"

"How come you going home?" Mindy asked.

"Remember, I told you I'm not feeling well? Do you want to stay here or go home with me?"

"She can stay here." Her father answered without looking up.

"Is that what you want, Mindy?" Emily asked.

"I want Thanksgivin' at Aunt Mary's house," Mindy answered.

"Okay, I'll come back Saturday afternoon to get you." Emily gave her a hug and walked out the door.

❖

She left the lights off in her house and went directly into the bathroom, stripped off her clothes, and stepped into the shower. She had managed to hold off most of the tears on her drive home, but they came out in uncontrollable sobs as the hot water ran over her. She slid down to the floor of the shower, onto her knees. Sorrow overtook her as her tears mixed with the water from the shower and disappeared down the drain.

When she was sure she had no more tears left in her body, she dried herself off and crawled into bed without bothering with her nightshirt. She fell into a fitful sleep from exhaustion, filled with random dreams of hurt and betrayal.

CHAPTER TWENTY-NINE

Emily woke with the sun the next morning. Her eyelids felt like they were held together with glue and her head drummed out a steady beat. The events of the previous evening came rushing back to her, and for a moment she thought she might puke. She no longer had any parents. Mom was dead and Dad didn't want anything to do with her. *What am I going to do? I am alone in the world.* No, you aren't, she argued with herself.

"You have Andi and you have Mindy," she said out loud. But what if Dad wouldn't let Mindy come back home with her? What if he hated her that much? *What if I show up at his house on Saturday and he won't even let me in?*

This wasn't right. Wasn't fair. She'd finally found herself only to lose her father. It would have been easier to just go on pretending to be something she wasn't, and hadn't ever truly been. *This sucks.* With that, the tears began to flow again and continued until Emily fell back asleep.

The sound of her cell phone shook her awake hours later. Disoriented, she wasn't sure where she had even left her phone the night before. It must be in her pants pocket on the floor in the bathroom. She decided to let it ring and made no move to get it. She wasn't in the mood to talk to anyone.

She wanted to stay in bed longer, but her screaming bladder was in charge. She caught a glimpse of herself in the bathroom mirror. Red, swollen eyes looked back at her. Hair stuck out in all directions. Guess it wasn't a good idea to go to bed with wet, uncombed hair. *Today you look as ugly as you feel.*

She kicked the clothes on the floor off to the side on her way out of the bathroom. Slipping into underwear, sweatpants, and a clean T-shirt, she eyed the bed but decided on a cup of coffee instead of going back to sleep.

"Hurry up," she yelled at the coffeemaker and poured herself a cup before the pot was full. She took a gulp of the coffee—black—and burnt her mouth. "Damn it! Fuck it all to hell." She stirred in her usual milk and sugar, then plopped down on the couch in the living room and turned on the TV. Floats from the Macy's Thanksgiving Day Parade flickered by without her taking much notice.

Her thoughts drifted to Andi, spending Thanksgiving Day with her family. She couldn't call her, and she wasn't even sure she wanted to talk to Andi right now, anyway. She'd never felt so alone and she was going to wallow in it for a good long while.

She finished her coffee and ignored the hunger pangs in her empty stomach. Her cell phone rang three more times; she could barely hear it from the couch, but that just made it easier to ignore. Random tears fell throughout the course of the day as her thoughts became almost too much to bear.

It was dark outside when Emily gave in to her growling stomach and poured a bowl of Cheerios. She sat in the silence of her empty house at the kitchen table to eat her supper. Alone.

Emily crawled back into bed and pulled the covers up around her, a box of tissues close by. Sleep came in spurts as she dozed and woke throughout the night.

Friday passed pretty much the same way Thursday had. Her cell phone continued to ring throughout the day and she continued to ignore it. Saturday morning Emily showered and dressed. After she grabbed her cell phone and car keys from her pants pocket, she deposited the dirty clothes in the laundry hamper and headed out the door.

In a booth at a nearby diner, she listened to the messages on her phone. One was from Mindy wishing her a "Merry Thanksgiving." Emily smiled at that one. The rest of the messages were from Andi. The first one said, "I wanted to call and make sure you got there all right. I miss you. Give me a call before you go to bed. I want to hear your voice." The last messages sounded more frantic. The last one said, "Emily, I'm getting really worried about you. I've called you several times now and I haven't heard back. Please call and let me know you're all right. I tried to find your dad's phone number to call him, but I couldn't. Please call me as soon as you get this."

Emily's breakfast arrived as she listened to the rest of Andi's messages. She realized she should have called her to let her know what had happened. She opened the contact list on her phone and hit Andi's number.

It was answered on the first ring. "Emily? Are you all right? Is everything okay?" The panic in Andi's voice was obvious.

"I'm sorry I didn't call sooner. I'm okay. Well, sort of okay. It didn't go too good with my father." Emily started to explain.

Andi interrupted her. "I'm sorry it didn't go the way you wanted it to, but I was panicked here. You couldn't pick up a phone and call me?" Emily heard the emotion build in Andi's voice. A mixture of frustration, relief, and anger poured through the phone. "I didn't know if you were dead in a ditch somewhere or what the hell to think. I spent more than two days worried sick over you."

"I'm sorry," Emily started.

"If this is the way you treat someone that you claim to have feelings for, I would hate to think how you treat someone that you don't care about. I am so hurt and pissed right now that I don't even want to talk to you." The line went dead.

Emily stared at the phone in her hand. She started to call Andi back but hung up before she finished. *Oh my God. Shit. Damn. Damn. Damn.* She'd blown it. So stupid. She was so caught up in her own pain that she didn't even think about what this was like for Andi. What an idiot. She'd have to figure out how to make this right. She couldn't lose her.

She pushed her breakfast aside, laid money on the table, and left, driving aimlessly for a while before pointing her car in the direction of Rochester to pick up Mindy. She was shaking by the time she pulled into her father's driveway. She sat in the car, certain that she was going to throw up. She closed her eyes and swallowed hard several times, trying to clear the feeling.

Without warning, her car door was opened from the outside. Startled, she looked up and saw her father standing there. She opened her mouth but no words came out.

William Sanders leaned down toward his daughter. "Can you come in so we can talk?"

She nodded and slid out of the seat. Together they walked into the house.

Emily sat in the rocking chair. "Where's Mindy?" she managed to ask, trying to keep her voice steady. Not sure if she succeeded.

Her father sat on the couch. "She's across the street at Lauren's house. I wanted to talk to you alone." He ran a hand across his chin. "I wanted to say I'm sorry. I didn't react very well when you told me, well, when you told me *what* you told me." He cleared his throat. "That you're gay. I'm not going to pretend that I understand it. But you're still my daughter and I love you."

Emily met her father's eyes. "Why the change of heart?"

"I've had a few days to think about it. To let it sink in. I don't know much about why someone's gay, but I do know you. I know you're a good person, and if you're gay it doesn't change that. I have a question about this, though."

"What?"

"Have you always been gay and you didn't tell me? Or is this new?"

"I guess I've always been gay but didn't even admit it to

myself until recently. So the realization is a fairly new thing. But when I did figure it out, I felt like a weight had been lifted off my shoulders. It's a lot of work hiding from yourself. I didn't want to hide from you too. That's why I told you." Emily decided not to tell him anything about Andi yet. She needed to make sure that she hadn't destroyed that completely.

"All your mother and I wanted for you girls was to be happy. Mindy seemed to be born with built-in happiness. Not so much for you. You've had your share of struggles and heartache. If part of that is because you're gay, and you have that part figured out now, then I guess I can live with that." He leaned back in his chair. "I'm assuming you haven't told Mindy yet."

"No, I haven't. I'm not sure she would understand."

"Mindy might surprise you, but I'll let you decide the best time to tell her. I just want you to know that, no matter what, I love you."

Relief washed over Emily like a wave. She hadn't lost her father after all. "I love you too, Dad."

❖

Mindy talked nonstop for the first half hour of the ride home. Emily suggested that they listen to the radio for a while and she let Mindy turn the dial until she found a station she liked. Mindy sang along with every song she knew, and she seemed to know most of them.

Emily knew that she had to keep her attention on driving. The traffic was fairly heavy and the last thing she needed was to get into an accident. Her mind kept wandering back to Andi. The relief she felt about her father's change of heart was overshadowed by her worry about having hurt Andi. She just wasn't sure how to make it right, but she knew she had to do it as soon as possible. Trying to fix it over the telephone wasn't an option. It had to be done face-to-face.

Emily pulled into the driveway. "I'll help you get your stuff and then I'm going to run over to Andi's house for a little while," she told Mindy.

"I wanna go too!"

"Not this time, Mindy. I need to talk to Andi about something, so please, help me out and find something to do or watch TV until I get back. Okay? Please."

"Okay, okay." Her irritation was obvious. Emily made sure she was settled before heading over to Andi's.

Emily was relieved to see Andi's car parked in the driveway. She took several deep breaths to try to calm herself and rang the doorbell, her heart in her throat. The door opened and Andi stood in front of her. The screen door separated them.

Emily pulled the screen open. "I am *so* sorry. I'm a jerk. Can I come in?" Emily's words came out in a rush. Andi stepped back to let her pass. Emily started again as soon as she entered the house. "Please forgive me. I wasn't thinking clearly."

Andi walked past her to the living room. She didn't say a word.

Emily followed. *I am not going to cry. Don't cry. Don't look pathetic. Just tell her your feelings.* "I'm so sorry I hurt you. I don't want to lose you." A tear escaped. She wiped it roughly away. "Please say something."

Nothing.

"Andi, please." She was willing to beg if she needed to.

"What the hell were you thinking? What the hell do you think went through my mind when I couldn't get ahold of you?"

"I wasn't thinking."

"No. I guess not."

At least she was talking to her.

"I was scared something had happened to you and no one knew to tell me."

Emily hadn't even considered that. She really was a thoughtless ass. How was she ever going to make up for this?

"Emily, if we're going to be together it has to be through

everything, not only when things are going good for you. If something bad happens, you need to share it with me. Not hide away. I can't take that." Andi turned her head to the side and Emily could tell that she was also struggling not to cry. She composed herself and continued, "We have to be there for each other. If I have a bad day, I want to be able to share it with you too. It's all or nothing, Emily. Do you get that?"

Emily nodded. She swallowed back the tears. "Yes, that's what I want too. I've never had that before and I was stupid. I'm so sorry I worried you."

"You aren't going to lose me, but it scares me if you're going to run when things get tough."

"I won't. I promise."

"God, Emily." This time Andi did let the tears fall. She turned her back. "Damn." The frustration obvious in her voice. She clenched her hands into fists.

Emily walked to her. She slipped her arms around her waist and rested her head against Andi's back. "Please forgive me."

Andi stepped out of her arms. "I need some time here, Emily."

Emily was at a loss for what to do next. "Do you want me to leave?" *Please say no.*

"No." Andi turned toward her.

Emily let out a breath that she didn't know she'd been holding.

"Please don't be mad." It was all she could think to say.

"I'm not mad. Don't you understand? I'm hurt. Hurt that you didn't feel you could talk to me. Hurt that you shut me out."

"Andi, so much of this is new to me. My feelings for you are so strong. My father's reaction was devastating to me. I didn't know how to respond. How to tell you. How to deal with it." She struggled to explain.

❖

So many feelings coursed through Andi at the same time that she had trouble sorting them out. She was hurt, she was angry, but most of all she was relieved. Relieved that Emily was all right. When her phone calls had gone unanswered, she was sure something must have happened, sure Emily must have been hurt or worse. She could think of no other reason for the silence she had gotten in response to her worried phone messages.

She wanted to hug Emily, to feel her arms around her, to know that she was safe. But at the same time she wanted to scream at her for making her worry when one single phone call would have alleviated the whole situation.

"Can we just sit down and talk?" Emily asked.

"Maybe it would be better if you left," Andi answered. She needed some time alone. Needed to calm down. Needed...what? She needed Emily, that's what. She knew that without a doubt. But did Emily need her? Emily had decided to handle her feelings on her own, without Andi. Maybe that was the way Emily operated. If that was the case, this wasn't going to work.

She needed some time to think.

CHAPTER THIRTY

A ndi and Emily hadn't talked at all by the time school started back up on Monday, and Andi was miserable. She missed Emily and was ready to talk. She believed she had relayed her feelings adequately on Saturday and didn't feel the need to explain further. She did have a few questions for Emily, though. Above all, she knew her life was better with Emily in it and was eager to get back to that. She stopped in Emily's room before lunch. But Emily wasn't there. She wasn't in the teachers' lounge either. Andi had a meeting after school with a parent, so she thought maybe she would stop by Emily's house after that.

She only had to wait a couple of seconds after ringing the bell for Emily to answer. Emily stepped forward as if she was going to hug Andi and then must have thought better of it.

"Can I come in?" Andi asked.

"Of course." Emily stepped back to let her pass.

"Can we talk?"

Emily nodded.

They both found seats in the living room on the couch but didn't sit too close.

"I'm so sor—" Emily started at the same time Andi spoke.

"I would like—"

"Go ahead," Emily said, with a nod.

"I wanted to see if we could clear this up. I miss you."

"I miss you too, and I'm so sorry."

"I know you are," Andi said. She wanted to move closer and wrap her arms around Emily but needed to know a few things first. "I need to know what went on with your dad and why you didn't call me."

Emily took a deep breath and explained what had happened and how it made her feel. "I wallowed in my own pain and like a fool felt alone. Andi, you need to realize that I have never had a relationship like this before—a relationship with someone who really cares about me and would worry about me. I didn't take that into account. That was wrong, and that was selfish. I know that now. I will never let anything like that happen again." Her voice shook and Andi knew she was being sincere.

"Emily, do you believe I care for you?"

"Of course I do."

"Then why wouldn't you let me be there for you?"

"Because I felt worthless, unlovable, a burden. I'm not saying any of this makes sense. I'm just telling you how I felt and why I thought it was best to be alone in my suffering."

Andi put her hand on Emily's knee, realizing how much she'd missed touching her. "Em, you could never be a burden to me. Your pain is my pain."

Emily swiped at the tears that leaked from her eyes. She nodded, and Andi knew her well enough to know that the tears would start in earnest if Emily spoke again. She moved closer and wrapped her arms around Emily. Maybe she had overreacted. Maybe she should have been more understanding of what Emily had been going through. All she knew for sure was that Emily was very important to her, and she couldn't bear the thought of them being apart any longer.

"I'm sorry too, Em."

Emily leaned into Andi and hugged her tightly. "I love you," she said.

These were the words Andi had been waiting to hear. The

words that told her how Emily truly felt. She kissed Emily full on the mouth. "Oh, Emily, I love you too."

They stayed wrapped around each other for what seemed like a long time. Andi wanted to stay like this forever.

❖

"Do you want to go start a fire?" Emily asked Andi.

"I would love to start a fire with you, but won't Mindy be home soon?"

"She won't be home for a few hours, and I meant a fire in the actual fireplace. I've only used it once since moving in, and I was by myself. I would love to sit in front of it with you."

Andi led Emily by the hand to the cove off the living room. Emily sat on the floor and rested her back against the love seat. Andi lit a match and held it to the corner of the starter log on the bottom of the pile of wood in the fireplace. The log caught and the fire slowly spread.

Andi sat on the floor next to Emily, the soft rug protecting them from the hardwood floor below. She put her arm around Emily, and Emily cuddled close against her.

Emily let out a contented sigh.

"My words exactly," Andi said.

The fire leaped to life in front of them and Emily began to feel its warmth. She also felt another kind of warmth that was far stronger than the fire before her. She raised her head to the person who caused the fire within by her mere presence. She kissed Andi on the cheek and then full on the mouth. A bit of rearranging and Emily was on her back, in Andi's arms, looking up at her. The firelight danced in Andi's eyes.

Andi bent her head, and lips met lips. She opened her mouth and allowed Emily's exploring tongue inside. Their tongues danced together in a slow waltz. Andi's hand tugged at Emily's shirt, pulling it from the waistband that held it captive. Her hands slid over the bare skin on Emily's stomach and moved upward, leaving a trail like burning embers in its wake until, at last, it reached Emily's breast. The fingers moved deftly across the material of Emily's bra, causing her nipples to stand at attention. Andi's fingers lingered there, taking possession of the hard nipple. Emily gasped as Andi's hand left her breast and in one swift motion slipped down her body and inside the front of her pants. Emily unzipped them, giving Andi's hand the freedom to move.

Andi's hand slid first over Emily's underpants, the fabric already soaked, then under the silky material, skin to skin. Andi's fingers moved through the wetness and she stroked Emily with a steady rhythm that seemed to match the rapid beating of Emily's heart.

Emily raised her hips to meet Andi's hand stroke for stroke. Over and over again. The pressure inside Emily increased to a blinding level. A small cry escaped her lips and tears leaked as she squeezed her eyes closed. Her body rocked with her climax. Andi increased the speed and pressure of her movements for a few moments more and then stopped, letting Emily's movement dictate what she needed.

Emily could hear the pounding of Andi's heart as she laid her head against her lover's chest, trying to catch her breath. She only realized her cheeks were wet with her own tears when Andi wiped them away.

"I don't know where the waterworks came from," Emily said, when she was able to speak. "I'm not crying. It's just so emotional for me to be with you. I am so in love with you."

"I know." Andi leaned down and kissed where the trail of tears had been. "Believe me, I know."

"Oh, and by the way"—Emily looked into Andi's eyes—"wow!"

Andi smiled and kissed Emily gently on the mouth as the fire roared in front of them.

EPILOGUE

H ow about this one?" Andi asked.

Emily looked the tree up and down. "No. It's too perfect." She continued down the row of evergreens.

"What do you mean, it's too perfect?" Andi asked as she caught up with her.

"It doesn't have character. It needs a few flaws to give it character." Emily pulled another Christmas tree from the row to get a better look at it. It had more branches on one side than the other and a slight bend in the trunk. "See how much character this tree has?"

"I'm beginning to see how much character you have." Andi smiled.

Emily swatted at her.

"Okay, okay. So, is this the tree you want?"

"What do you think?" Emily wanted it to be a joint decision.

"I think it's beautiful and has a lot of character." Andi wrapped her arms around Emily from behind. "I think we should get it," she said close to Emily's ear, sending shivers down Emily's back. She pushed down the urge to turn in Andi's arms and kiss her full on the mouth. There would be plenty of time for that later.

"Thank you," Emily said.

"For what?"

"For letting me get a tree with personality and for loving me."

"Loving you is the easy part." Andi gave her a tight squeeze before letting her go. "I'll go tell the guy we want this one."

Thirty minutes later they were setting the tree up in Emily's house. "Is that straight?" Andi asked Emily.

"A little more to the left."

Andi adjusted the tree.

"No, no, too much."

Another adjustment.

"No, it still doesn't look right. Try turning it a little." Emily stood back and tilted her head. "You know, I'm thinking that the tree has a little too much personality to be straight. Kind of like you." She smiled.

"Oh, nice," Andi said, letting go of the tree. She grabbed Emily around the waist and pulled her in close for a kiss.

Emily leaned back out of the reach of her mouth. "Wait. This isn't official," she said.

A look of confusion crossed Andi's face. "What do you mean it isn't official?"

"Well, it's getting close to Christmas, and you want to kiss me."

"I'm not seeing where you're going with this."

Emily pulled out of Andi's embrace and held up one finger. She looked through one of the cardboard boxes that she'd brought up from the basement earlier. She pushed aside various Christmas decorations until she found what she was looking for. She held it above her head.

"Mistletoe," Andi said.

"Now it's official, so get over here and kiss me."

"My God, you're bossy."

"You're right. That was a little bossy," Emily said. "Let me rephrase." She cleared her throat. "Get over here and kiss me—please."

"That's better." Andi pulled her back into her arms. She gave Emily a tender kiss on the lips.

Emily pulled Andi in tighter and returned the kiss with much more passion and hunger. "How was that?" Emily asked.

"Oh, I like it when it's official. I like it a lot."

"I am going to hang this up over there." Emily pointed to the doorway leading down the hall. "So we can be official over there. In fact, I think I will get a whole bunch of mistletoe and hang it all over the house. Your house too. That way we can be official all over the place."

Emily used a stool to tack up the mistletoe. She felt the warmth of Andi's arms around her and Andi's body against her back when she stepped down.

Andi kissed her on the neck. "Got any plans for Christmas?" Andi said. "'Cause I can think of a few ways I'd like to spend it."

Emily turned to face her. "Actually, I do have plans for Christmas that I was hoping would involve you."

"Oh yeah? Tell me."

"It's not what you think."

"And just how do you know what I'm thinking," Andi said, with a grin.

"I would venture to guess that you are thinking about you and me and no clothes and a bed and—"

"Okay," Andi interrupted. "Maybe you do know what I'm thinking. What are you thinking?"

"I told my dad about us when I talked to him on the phone yesterday," Emily said.

Andi looked concerned. She waited for Emily to continue.

"He said he was happy for me. He already knew a lot about you, not that you're my girlfriend, but Mindy happened to tell him that you are her *best friend* and you know how she loves to talk about her *best friends*."

"I do indeed." Andi smiled. "So, your dad was all right with me being in your life?"

"He seemed to be. He invited you to go there with us for Christmas. What would you think about that?"

"Hmm. Okay, I thought about it and I want to be wherever you are for Christmas." She kissed Emily's nose. "'Cause I happen to love you."

"You do?"

"I do."

"Well, that works out great, then, because I happen to love you too." She looked up. "We're still standing under the mistletoe. Want to kiss me again?"

Andi brought her mouth to Emily's and kissed her deeply. They were still wrapped in each other's arms and their own little world when the front door opened and closed. They didn't hear Mindy come into the house or into the room.

"What? You are kissing a girl?" Mindy exclaimed, her eyes and mouth open wide.

Emily quickly pulled out of Andi's embrace.

Dead silence.

Mindy spoke again. "What, are you g-gay or something?"

Emily looked at Andi.

Andi nodded.

"Yes, Mindy," Emily said softly. "I'm gay. I'm gay, and I love Andi." She held her breath waiting for Mindy's response.

"Oh. Okay." Mindy proceeded to take her off her scarf and mittens.

"Are you sure you're okay with this? Do you have any questions or anything?" Emily watched her little sister.

"It's fine. My best friend, Ellen Degeneres, is g-gay, for g-g-goodness sake. What the big deal?"

Emily was relieved, but wasn't quite sure her little sister understood. "So, you don't have any problem with me kissing Andi or being gay. You understand what it means?"

"Yep. You're a girl and Andi's a girl and you love each other and are gay together. I not a little kid, you know. Can we d-d-decorate the tree now?" She brought her attention to the evergreen in the corner. "It's p-p-perfect." She smiled her bright, crooked smile.

Emily pulled Andi back into her arms and hugged her tight, giving her a quick kiss on the mouth. It was going to be a great holiday.

About the Author

Creativity for Joy Argento started young. She was only five, growing up in Syracuse, New York, when she picked up a pencil and began drawing animals. These days she calls Rochester home, and oil paints are her medium of choice. Her award-winning art has found its way into homes around the globe.

Writing came later in life for Joy. Her love of lesbian romance inspired her to try her hand at writing, and she found her first self-published novels well received. She is thrilled to be a part of the Bold Strokes family and has enjoyed their books for years.

Joy has three grown children who are making their own way in the world and two grandsons who are the light of her life.

Visit her website at www.joyargento.com.

Books Available From Bold Strokes Books

Emily's Art and Soul by Joy Argento. When Emily meets Andi Marino she thinks she's found a new best friend, but Emily doesn't know that Andi is fast falling in love with her. Caught up in exploring her sexuality, will Emily see the only woman she needs is right in front of her? (978-1-163555-355-0)

Escape to Pleasure: Lesbian Travel Erotica, edited by Sandy Lowe and Victoria Villasenor. Join these award-winning authors as they explore the sensual side of erotic lesbian travel. (978-1-163555-339-0)

Music City Dreamers by Robyn Nyx. Music can bring lovers together. In Music City, it can tear them apart. (978-1-163555-207-2)

Ordinary is Perfect by D. Jackson Leigh. Atlanta marketing superstar Autumn Swan's life derails when she inherits a country home, a child, and a very interesting neighbor. (978-1-163555-280-5)

Royal Court by Jenny Frame. When royal dresser Holly Weaver's passionate personality begins to melt Royal Marine Captain Quincy's icy heart, will Holly be ready for what she exposes beneath? (978-1-163555-290-4)

Strings Attached by Holly Stratimore. Rock star Nikki Razer always gets what she wants, but when she falls for Drew McNally, a music teacher who won't date celebrities, can she convince Drew she's worth the risk? (978-1-163555-347-5)

The Ashford Place by Jean Copeland. When Isabelle Ashford inherits an old house in small-town Connecticut, family secrets, a shocking discovery, and an unexpected romance complicate her plan for a fast profit and a temporary stay. (978-1-163555-316-1)

Treason by Gun Brooke. Zoem Malderyn's existence is a deadly threat to everyone on Gemocon, and Commander Neenja KahSandra must find a way to save the woman she loves from having to make the ultimate sacrifice. (978-1-163555-244-7)

A Wish Upon a Star by Jeannie Levig. Erica Cooper has learned to depend on only herself, but when her new neighbor, Leslie Raymond, befriends Erica's special needs daughter, the walls protecting Erica's heart threaten to crumble. (978-1-163555-274-4)

Answering the Call by Ali Vali. Detective Sept Savoie returns to the streets of New Orleans, as do the dead bodies from ritualistic killings, and she does everything in her power to bring their killers to justice while trying to keep her partner, Keegan Blanchard, safe. (978-1-163555-050-4)

Friends Without Benefits by Dena Blake. When Dex Putman gets the woman she thought she always wanted, she soon wonders if it's really love after all. (978-1-163555-349-9)

Invalid Evidence by Stevie Mikayne. Private Investigator Jil Kidd is called away to investigate a possible killer whale, just when her partner Jess needs her most. (978-1-163555-307-9)

Pursuit of Happiness by Carsen Taite. When attorney Stevie Palmer's client reveals a scandal that could derail Senator Meredith Mitchell's presidential bid, their chance at love may be collateral damage. (978-1-163555-044-3)

Seascape by Karis Walsh. Marine biologist Tess Hansen returns to Washington's isolated northern coast, where she struggles to adjust to small-town living while courting an endowment from Brittany James for her orca research center. (978-1-163555-079-5)

Second In Command by VK Powell. Jazz Perry's life is disrupted and her career jeopardized when she becomes personally involved with the case of an abandoned child and the child's competent but strict social worker, Emory Blake. (978-1-163555-185-3)

Taking Chances by Erin McKenzie. When Valerie Cruz and Paige Wellington clash over what's in the best interest of the children in Valerie's care, the children may be the ones who teach them it's worth taking chances for love. (978-1-163555-209-6)